Holy Seduction

A NOVEL BY JESSICA A. ROBINSON

Holy Seduction

A NOVEL BY JESSICA A. ROBINSON

Peace In The Storm Publishing, LLC

Acknowledgements

I would like to thank my lord and savior, Jesus Christ. You've opened so many doors for me. My dream wouldn't have been possible without you.

Gabriel and Michael, thank you for being the best brothers a girl could have. I love you so much.

To my grandparents, **Ann, Nate, Willard, and Ruth.** I love you so much for everything you've done and continue to do for me.

To **Pastor Denis, First Lady Sandra Robinson, and the Entire Everlife Worship Center Family:** Your support has been tremendous. Thank you for always believing in me and for all your prayers.

To **Dean, Deborah, Crystal, Fran, Gerald, Natalie, Amber, and Danny. I love you all.**

To my wonderful all-star editor, **Rhonda Crowder,** thanks for taking the time out and really teaching me some valuable things about the craft of writing. I appreciate all you've done for me. I can't wait to see your masterpiece hit the shelves.

Special thanks and appreciation go to **Davida Baldwin, Leila Jefferson, and Tifany Berry.** Thanks for helping to pull everything together.

To **Carnival: Brandon, Jay, and Sean.** Thank you for truly having my back at all times and being my brothers for real. I'm blessed to have you in my life. This is our year! ☺ "Population of Invisible People"…coming July 28!

To **Crystal, Stacia, Jacques, Keya, Lillie, Monica, Lisa, Shannon, Jonathan, Kristen, DJ, Ryan, Nicci, Denis Jr., Taylor, Chessie, Liz, Penny, Janelle, Sam, Allyson, Cee-Cee, Daijah, Attim, Briana, Brandi, Sean, Silas, Savon, Nicholas, Jovan, Christopher, Kayla, Brandon aka Peanut, Londen, A.J., and Amir** Thanks for being wonderful cousins to me. I love you.

To **David A. Robinson**, not only are you my cousin, you are my talented business partner. God has so many things in store for you, I can't wait to see.

To **Matia,** I love you sis…call me sometimes. Lol ☺

To my Godsons and Goddaughter, **T.J., Cameron, and Brenda**…I love you so much.

To my fabulous friends: **Sarah, Jen, Jada, Travelle, Tasha, Maurice, Lauren, Robert, Jalana, Jonai, Doran, Leann, Cornelius, Dave, Ben, and Summer.** Thanks for your genuine friendship.

Dorothy, Harley, Kylie, Kelis, and Isaiah, I love you all so much. I thank you for being there for me through the thick and thin. I truly appreciate all of the things you've done for me and I appreciate the love you've shown me. Tell the girls that they can "spend over forever" real soon! LOL ☺

Special shout outs to: **Js Queen, Mahogani, Essence, Kariymah, Tori, Bookbabe**

Special thanks to my sis **Canedra**. You've supported me from day one and I'm glad God allowed us to cross paths.

Thanks to **Martha Taylor, Arlene & Al Beaver, and Lois Hines**. I love you all. Thanks for being my support system.

Regina Perry, Tasha "Diva" Dendy, Happy Monroe, Calvin Allen, Lisa & Lorne Laney, Andrea Mahone, Monica Curry and Natalie Scott: I appreciate every positive word you've spoken into my life.

To **Elissa Gabrielle and the Peace in the Storm Family**, you go above and beyond for me so I thank you from the bottom of my heart. Thanks for taking my story and believing in it. You've made my dream a reality and this is just the beginning.

To **T. Styles, Charisse Washington, Jason Poole, and The Cartel Publications**. Thanks for truly making me feel like family. I appreciate all the love you've shown. **Mia aka Kalico Jones**, thanks for supporting me.

To fellow authors: **Tamara, Ebonee, S.D. Denny, Claudia, Cheryl, Jackie, Lorraine**: Let's make history. The world better get ready for the **STORM**.

To **Kevin Deane, Jason and Sandy Hollis:** Thank you for everything.

To **Literary Lovers Book Club, ASA, AAMBC, Sistah Confessions, Tamika Newhouse, Linda Herman, and Allyson Deese**. Thanks for your support. To **Ella Curry and Kisha Green**: Thanks for the interviews and continual exposure.

And to **YOU!** _____(your name), thanks for purchasing my debut novel. I hope you've really enjoy **Holy Seduction**. Thanks in advance for your love and support.

Until next time,
Jessica A. Robinson

Dedication

My debut novel is dedicated to both of my parents, Rev. Willard Dwight Robinson and Min. Marcella Robinson. Even though you are no longer present with me, I still feel you near me. All of the values, morals, and lessons you taught me are evident in my life today. I live to make you proud. I love you.

Chapter One

"Baby, it's nine o'clock. Don't you have somewhere to be?" Tyrone asked as he got up from the bed and put on his jeans. In a complete frenzy, Denise Tate jumped out of the bed and started gathering her clothes.

"I told my husband I would meet him for dinner at nine… I'll never make it in time," she said as she began to panic.

"Just hurry up, you'll make it in time to meet your husband," Tyrone reassured.

As Denise got the rest of her things, her mind began to wonder if her husband would question her whereabouts or smell the scent of another man on her skin. These kinds of questions drove her crazy so when she was creeping around so, instead of dwelling, she just dismissed them because, in her mind, her husband must never find out.

Tyrone walked over to the edge of the bed and sat down. "Denise, how long are you going to keep this up?" he asked.

She looked over at him as if she didn't know what he was talking about but she heard exactly what he said.

JESSICA A. ROBINSON

"Keep what up?" she asked with a confused look on her face.

"You know what I'm talking about. You promised me that you were going to leave him so we can be together."

"I am going to leave him! I told you that," Denise replied.

"Well, why am I still a secret?" Tyrone looked Denise straight in her eyes. Denise had her own problems so the last thing she needed was to be questioned by him. Just when things were good between them, Tyrone had to mess it up with asking questions. She felt like she was in jail being interrogated. When she first hooked up with him, they agreed that there would be "no strings attached." That was definitely what they had settled upon in the beginning but, like all the other men Denise encountered, they all wanted something more. All of her former lovers wanted more than what she was willing to give. She simply wanted sex while they wanted a relationship. So, like all the others, Denise knew she would eventually have to cut Tyrone off. But, somehow, cutting him off hadn't been that easy. He was everything she looked for in a lover: tall, dark complexion, beautiful muscle tone, and the moves to make a true sista moan. She really did like Tyrone but wouldn't dare mess up what she's got going on at home to be with him.

"Tyrone, you know I care about you a lot and want to be with you, but right now is not a good time to break the news to my husband. I mean, he is at the height of his career and leaving right now will mess him up." Denise put on her jacket.

"I love you so much, Denise. I just want us to be together. I'm tired of sneaking around and keeping everything a secret." He got up and pulled Denise close to him.

"Don't worry. He'll know about us in due time." Denise kissed him softly on his lips on her way out of the door. She figured telling Tyrone what he wanted to hear

14

would pacify him for a little while longer. But, in all actuality, she had no intentions of leaving her husband since she became too accustomed to the furs, shopping sprees, vacations, and most importantly, the 6,000 square foot house her husband had built especially for her.

She would have to be almost insane to mess all of that up.

Denise drove her black Lexus RX 330 SUV as fast as she could to meet her husband for dinner. As her tires began to hit the thin layer of rain that fell on the highway, she recalled the first time she met Tyrone Banks at a benefit dinner the church held for the homeless.

"How are you, Miss Tate?" a voice called from behind her.

"Hi. How are you?" she asked as she extended her hand and shook his.

"Oh. I'm sorry. My name is Tyrone Banks," he said as he gripped her hand.

"It's very nice to meet you," she replied.

"This is a nice dinner," he said as he looked around the room at everyone who seemed to be enjoying the evening.

"Yes. This is a dinner my husband puts together every year to help the homeless," she continued.

Tyrone's mouth dropped to the ground. "Your husband? You're telling me that you're married?" he asked as if he was in some kind of shock.

"Yes, that's my husband. Why are you so surprised?" she asked as he picked up her hand and examined her four carat diamond ring that sparkled as the light hit it.

"I'm just surprised that you're married because you don't look like someone who is spoken for," Tyrone replied. "Honestly, I thought you were Pastor Tate's younger sister, not his wife." Denise smiled from ear to ear.

JESSICA A. ROBINSON

"Oh that's so sweet of you, Tyrone. Your wife must be a very lucky woman," Denise stated, trying to figure out if he was also taken.

"What wife? I'm not married. I am a very single man," he announced. Tyrone's being single really turned Denise on.

"Well, my husband is calling me but I hope to see you again," she said as she turned to walk away.

Tyrone grabbed her hand. "Oh, don't worry. We'll see each other again." She later learned through conversation that Tyrone was a contractor who lived in Austintown and worked on some of the biggest construction projects in the city of Youngstown, Ohio. He also told her he owned his own condo and basically stayed to himself, which was perfect for her. She could tell by the way he licked his lips and bit down on his bottom one that he was attracted to her. Denise felt the feeling was mutual and it would only be a matter of time until he became hers.

Denise pulled into the parking lot of *The Upstairs* and glanced down at her silver Movado watch. She managed to make it to the restaurant from Tyrone's condo in record time. Even though she was late, she still had made it to the restaurant in less than twenty minutes. Before she got out of her truck, Denise checked her reflection in the mirror. She smoothed a few pieces of hair that had slipped out of place and applied a fresh coat of lip gloss. *He'll never know,* she thought to herself as she walked in the upscale establishment.

"Hey baby. Where have you been? I was starting to get worried," Randy said as he got up from the table and took off Denise's coat.

"I'm sorry, honey. I was running a little late. One of the ladies from the church called the house and needed prayer so I prayed for her," Denise lied. She knew beyond a shadow of a doubt her husband wouldn't question her when thinking she was doing the Lord's work. So, in that, her lies were always secure. Denise always had a for sure alibi if she threw the Lord up in it.

"You know what? Not only are you beautiful and my wife, you are truly a help to me." He kissed Denise's hand. It was in those moments Denise wished her husband wouldn't be as soft since his continual charm added to her guilt.

"Oh you're so sweet," she answered.

"I'm so glad that we're alone. We don't get to do this that often enough," Randy said as the waiter brought them their drinks.

"Yeah, sometimes it's hard to get together with you being a pastor, but I understand you have to do your job," she answered.

The fact that Denise didn't spend much time with Randy didn't bother her at all instead it just gave her more time to do what she wanted to do. Most women wouldn't like all of the free time she had, but she absolutely loved it. She didn't believe in being around her husband every waking moment of the day, and she didn't expect him to be stuck up underneath her butt all day either. Their arrangement worked out perfectly fine for her and she was content with the way things were.

"Baby, I thank you for being so understanding. That was one of the things I fell in love with and I promise you, we're going to spend more time together," Randy said as he looked at the woman he adored so much. As far as he was concerned, his wife was the epitome of perfection.

"Well, I can't wait for that day," Denise smiled.

Randy reached inside his coat pocket, pulled out a box, and told her to open it. Denise's mouth dropped to the floor. He presented a two thousand dollar, platinum tennis bracelet with enough "ice" to put in everyone's drinks at the restaurant.

"Randy, it's so beautiful. You shouldn't have," she said as she tried to remain humble as possible while he reached over the table and put it on her wrist.

"Baby, you deserve the best. Besides, you've been talking about this for months." Randy smiled as the bracelet sparkled on her arm.

"Thank you, Randy. I love it. I love you." Denise leaned over the table and kissed Randy then her cell phone rang.

"Who is that?" Randy asked as a weird expression was on his wife's face.

"Oh…uhhh…this is Sis Daphne on the phone. I'm just surprised because she never calls me," Denise answered. "I'm going to take this. I'll be right back." She got up from the table and walked toward the bathroom area.

When she looked at her caller I.D. screen, she realized it was Jackson Mitchell. He just so happened to be a blast from Denise's past so she just had to take his call.

"I can't believe you called me," Denise answered with a huge grin.

"You know I'm always thinking about you. How've you been?"

"I'm better now you're on the phone," Denise replied and he chuckled.

"Well. Guess what? I have a surprise for you."

"Oooh, what is it?" Denise asked with anticipation in her voice.

"I'm in town for two days."

"You're here? Please don't play around with me. Are you serious?"

"I'm serious, baby girl. I'm here for a couple days trying a case and I want to spend some time with you," he explained while her husband waited.

"That would be nice."

"Well, how about you come out and play tonight?" Jackson continued.

18

"Sounds good to me. What time?" Denise asked as she looked down at her watch.

"How do ten sound?"

"Perfect. I'll see you then," she replied as she pressed the end button on her cell phone. She set a late night rendezvous with Jackson so all she needed was an excuse to get out of the house at such an odd hour. She walk into the ladies room to get her expressions together because she knew, once she hung up from him, she smiled like a Cheshire cat and Randy would definitely be suspicious as to why she grinned so hard.

"Baby, was everything alright with Sis Daphne?" Randy asked as she sat back down at the table.

"Everything's fine. She just needed some prayer," Denise replied.

"Oh. Okay," he responded as a short, thin, waitress came to the table to take their orders.

"Did you two decide on what you would like this evening?" she asked as she pulled out a notepad.

"Yes. I think I'll have a lobster tail and grilled vegetables," said Denise.

"I would like the T-bone steak and a baked potato, please," Randy followed before the waitress walked off and disappeared into the kitchen.

"So how were things at the church today?" Denise asked after taking a sip of her sweet tea.

"Things were good, babe, for the most part. I had a meeting with the maintenance department about some work that need to be done. I must admit, it started out a little rough but got better as time went on," he continued.

"What happened?"

"Some things need to be repaired and they're not done. I figured I would meet with them collectively to see what was going on. I learned from talking to everyone, they weren't fixing anything for trying to conserve on money."

"Why they doing that?"

"Honestly, I don't know. But, I told them there is more than enough money in our budget to make the necessary repairs. We have a 3.5 million dollar building and I'm sorry, certain things can't be fixed with duct tape and super glue."

"Please don't tell me that's what they used."

"Denise, I know it's hard to believe. But, I can show you what they tried to fix. It would make you laugh."

"I'm glad you got to the bottom of everything because that wouldn't have been good at all."

Over the course of their dinner, Denise and Randy talked about the rest of their day and, by the time the dessert menu was offered, they both turned it down claiming they were entirely too full. Then, Denise casually glanced at her watch and realized she needed to get going. So, she stretched her arms and let out a big yawn.

"Randy, it's getting kind of late. Are you ready?" She looked at her watch again. He agreed then signaled the waitress to settle the check. Once she completed the transaction and was tipped, they stood up then proceeded to exit.

While walking to the car, she brainstormed ways she could get out of the house. As she drove off, she decided to tell him she needed to take a quick trip over her best friend Terri's house. He would never suspect anything because they spent a lot of time together anyway. If he asked her why she was going over there so late, she figured she would just tell him Terri was having man problems and needed to talk.

Just as Denise turned on her CD player, her cell phone chirped, indicating she had an incoming text. She pressed the button on her Blackberry and saw it a message from Jackson. *I can't wait to see you*, it read. Instantly, she got butterflies in her stomach as if she was a young school girl talking to her first puppy dog crush. *I can't wait to see you either, I'll be there in an hour*, she answered him back before turning into her driveway. And, when she pulled in the garage, she realized Randy beat her home.

All she had to do was stick with her plan and everything would be fine. She would be free and clear to leave. As Denise opened the door to the house, the lights were dim and music played softly in the background. She stood still and looked around until she saw Randy coming down the steps, wearing her favorite pair of boxers.

"Denise, this is the second part of our evening," he said as he walked over and took off her coat. "All I want you to do is sit back, relax, and enjoy what I'm going to do for you." He smiled as she took a seat.

He undressed her slowly as well as kissed her neck and Denise began to enter into pure ecstasy since he did everything to please her. From there, he led her upstairs where a hot bubble bath awaited. Thoughts of meeting up with Jackson seemed to disappear as Randy took his time and bathed every inch of her body. She felt bad about standing him up but, after all, her husband finally wanted to spend time with her as oppose to work on his weekly sermon or go to sleep, so anyone else had to wait.

The next morning, Denise agreed to meet Jackson in his penthouse suite for brunch. She knew he would be a little pissed off about the night before but hoped the way she looked and the length of time since they last saw each other would force him to allow this little mishap to slide. He was a man with great power and prestige as well as one of the best lawyers this side of the Mississippi. He was also a very meticulous man who valued his time and hated to be late or cancel appointments. Since he already told her where he was staying, she didn't bother to call him. She just hopped on the elevator and rode it to the twelfth floor. When the doors opened, she realized his suite was the only one up there so she walked right up to the door and turned the knob.

"Denise. Long time no see." Jackson smiled as he watched her every move.

"I know. It's been a while." She walked up to him and kissed him.

"What? Like six months?" he responded while motioning for them to sit down.

"Yeah. It's been about that long." Denise set her Fendi purse on the coffee table. "You're still looking good," Jackson replied.

"You don't look too bad yourself," she said as he playfully smacked his lips. "I know I may be older than you but I know I still got it," he said in a cocky tone.

"You sure do." From that point on, the talking between them ceased. She missed his strong hands caressing her body and knew he desired the way she put it on him as well. Their relationship was a pretty erratic one, but it had been an arrangement that worked for the both of them. He was a busy lawyer who resided in Akron, Ohio and she was the first lady of a church, so they would try to see each other whenever they could. That type of freedom was perfect for Denise. She honestly liked Jackson and was even more attracted to the fact he wasn't so clingy. He gave her more than enough space but, when they were together, he made sure he gave her what she wanted. And, he spoiled Denise with more expensive gifts than she could handle. Most of the time, he gave her unbelievable amounts of money. That was also fine by her too. She figured his money was green just like everyone else's and, if all Jackson wanted was a little booty in return, she considered the money he gave her to be well within her rights to receive.

After they messed around for about two hours, they finally decided to partake in the brunch he'd ordered for them. Denise couldn't help but smile while being in Jackson's presence because he did everything he could to make her feel special.

"I'll tell you one thing, I surely missed being with you." Jackson picked up the last big, fat, juicy strawberry and fed it to Denise.

"I missed you too. I'm so glad you came to town."

"I had to come on business but getting to be with you made it worth my while," he replied as his phone alarm sounded off. "I almost forgot I have a preliminary court date with my client. I'm sorry to have to cut our afternoon short."

"It's okay. I understand you're in high demand," Denise teased while he started to put on his suit. In record time, he was dressed and on his way out the door.

"Feel free to stay for a while. Just shut the door when you leave."

"Okay. I will."

"Oh and, Denise, I left you something." He smiled as he walked out.

She hurried over to the nightstand and noticed a wad full of cash wrapped with a silk bow around it. She didn't even bother to count it because by the size, she knew it was at least a grand. Most women in her situation would feel as though they were prostituting themselves by messing around with Jackson but not Denise. She figured he just wanted to take care of her and that's exactly what she allowed him to do.

After Denise left the hotel, she called Terri to see if she was still at work. It was early enough in the day and since she was close to downtown, she would visit her. But, Terri ended up working from home that day so Denise went over to her house. Terri answered the door in her pajamas and her hair pulled back into a tight bun.

"Girl! Do you know it's almost four in the afternoon? Why aren't you dressed?"

"Since I was off, I didn't see the necessity in dressing up and wasting a perfectly good outfit. Besides, I've been working since this morning and had no time to think about anything else. I'm actually glad you came over though because I need to take a break," Terri said.

"You definitely need to take a break! You're always working hard."

"You know what I need right now?" Terri asked Denise while they walked through her living room and down three steps to the family room.

"What do you need? A man?" Denise asked as Terri smacked her arm with a document she carried in her hand.

"I need one of them in the worst way but I'm talking about a drink. Haven't had one in a while," she continued.

"I don't see why not. You got a full bar in your house. If I had one, I wouldn't have that problem," Denise replied.

"Yes you would. The name of your problem would be R to the A to the N to the D to the Y. You know your husband wouldn't even allow something like that."

"Okay. Maybe, I went a little too far, but I don't think he would trip about me drinking. He knew I used to drink when we first met."

"Yeah, he knows you used to drink. But, I bet he don't know you still drink all the time and be blazin' up too when you get a chance."

Denise giggled before she answered Terri. "What Randy doesn't know, won't hurt him."

"Whatever, cause, why you playing, Randy's the reason you stopped going out."

"Now, let me clarify one thing. I didn't stop because of him. I stopped because it could bring bad publicity to the church. Randy doesn't need that."

"Same thing."

"You know good and well I'm not the only one to blame. After you started law school we barely went out."

Terri stepped behind the bar and pulled out two glasses. "Whatever, Miss Thang. What you want to drink?"

"I'll take a Grey Goose and cranberry."

"Your favorite. I think I'll fix me a Long Island Ice Tea." Terri combined the liquor and juice, shook it up and then poured it into a tall, skinny glass.

"Thank you, barmaid." Denise put a straw in her drink and took a sip. As she consumed the contents she thought about how much fun she had when Terri did bartend. Terri had just graduated from Youngstown State University and was looking to make some extra money. With all the funds she'd received in scholarships and grants, it still wasn't enough to take care of her law school tuition and she didn't know how to do to make up the rest of the money until she browsed through "The Vindicator" one day and saw an advertisement. Terri made one phone call and the rest was history as she ended up becoming one of the best in the city.

"Remember when I worked at Choices?"

"How can I forget? I got in and drunk all night, for free, thanks to you." Denise handed her empty glass back to Terri.

"We used to have so much fun back then."

"I know," Denise replied.

"Seem like we've become what we always said we wouldn't."

"What you mean?" Denise raised her eyebrows in a confused manner.

"Boring adults..."

Denise smoothed a piece of her hair in the front and smacked her lips. "Your life may be boring, Ms. Attorney, but mines sure isn't."

"Shut up. I'm serious. When we were younger, we used to kick it hard and have the time of our lives. Now, with you bein' the first lady of Oakdale Baptist and me working all the time, we don't do anything fun."

"What do you suggest is the remedy, Oprah?"

"Let's kick it for a weekend. How about we take a little trip? Get away."

"I'm game. Name a time and place and I'm there."

"Whatever. You know Pastor Randy's got you on lockdown."

"He don't got nothin' on lockdown. He's so busy running the church he doesn't know what I do."

"You know he got a close and personal relationship with the Lord. You better hope he never tells him what you're really up to while he's tending to his flock."

"Shut up and fix me another one," Denise commented while they continued on for the rest of the afternoon in that manner. Denise even fell asleep and sobered up before going home while she still managed to make it there and in bed before Randy.

Chapter Two

Denise had not stepped foot in a gym for an entire two weeks and three days after drinking with Terri and couldn't believe she'd allowed herself to go that long without exercising, so when she woke up, she was more determined than ever to work-out.

"Honey, where are you going so early this morning?" Randy asked as he rolled over and saw Denise getting dressed.

"To the gym. It's been in while and that's so not like me."

"I know. I didn't even realize you hadn't been. Wish I could get to the gym but it's hard to find any free time. Then, when I finally have a moment, I usually try to get as much sleep as I can."

"I understand. Our congregation can make you tired. Well, I'll only be gone for a little while. You get some rest," Denise replied then leaned over the bed and kissed him.

"I won't be here when you get back but stop down at the church. Maybe we can have lunch together or something."

"Okay, babe, sounds like a plan." Denise walked over by the chaise lounge located in the sitting area of their bedroom and picked up her gym bag. She dropped her iPod in it and jogged down the steps then moved toward the keys on the wall in the kitchen. *What car do I feel like driving? I think I'm in a drop top Benz kind of mood.*

Denise grabbed the Tiffany ring holding the keys to the candy apple red Mercedes Randy brought her last Christmas and walked out the door. She smiled while looking at her absolute dream car sitting in its usual spot in the garage. It was beautiful and, from the moment she laid eyes on it, she had to have it. She knew it wasn't cheap but the price tag didn't matter to her. She wanted it and wouldn't be satisfied until he brought it for her. And from the moment she got it, she was the envy of all the women at church. They couldn't fathom the idea of driving in a brand spanking new, ninety-thousand dollar automobile while Denise believed they felt that way because their faith was too low. She thought lavish was the way God wanted her to live and so what if they couldn't understand it. They just had to deal with it, Denise thought as she pressed the unlock button and opened up the door.

I swear I love my life. I wouldn't trade places with anyone in this world. The way I see it, the only one that is qualified to live the life I'm living is me.

Whenever behind the wheel of her SLK, she felt in control and powerful, like she drove in a race car so she reached the gym in no time. As she pulled in the parking lot, her cell phone started to ring. She saw Tyrone's number flashing on the screen and pressed the *ignore* button. She hadn't spoken with or seen him in a while, which was okay with her since discovering she could only tolerate him in small spurts anyway. She knew he would probably be pissed off about his call going straight to voicemail, but she didn't have time to play twenty questions with him right before a work-out while she knew that's what their conversation would end up being once on the line with him. And, just as she placed her phone in her purse, she could hear it ringing.

It was Tyrone again.

Denise sucked her teeth and rolled her eyes. She couldn't understand, for the life of her, why he wouldn't get the hint. If he called right before that and couldn't get her, then what made him think he would be successful a second time. She enjoyed the sex but he was becoming more attached than she desired so she ignored him. However, when she opened the door to the gym, she bumped right into the very person she tried to avoid.

"Hey Tyrone. What are you doing here?"

"I just called you twice. Is something wrong with your phone?" he asked.

"Really?" Denise looked at her phone, acting like she didn't see them.

"For a minute, I thought you're trying to dodge me. It's been a while since we've seen each other." Tyrone stood with his arms crossed. "And to answer your question, I'm trying to come back and get myself in shape 'cause I've been slipping lately. Plus, I promised my cousin I would come back." Sweat beads started to run down the sides of his face. He grabbed a towel out of his bag and wiped them away.

"I'm not trying to avoid you. I've just been real busy that's all," she said

Tyrone, seeming satisfied with her answer, uncrossed his arms and then tugged on Denise's jacket in attempt to pull her closer but was unsuccessful because Denise planted her feet firmly in the ground so she didn't move an inch. She told him, time after time, how she felt about public displays of affection. But no matter how many times she said something, Tyrone still insisted on doing stupid things while they were out places. She was slowly beginning to believe he was slow or had attention deficit disorder because he couldn't follow directions to save his life.

"I was calling you because I am off today and wondered if we could get together for a romantic evening at my place."

"I'll have to check my schedule and get back to you," Denise replied and rolled her eyes, even though she didn't have anything planned.

"What schedule do you have to check? You don't work so you should be free."

"Tyrone, little do you know, my schedule is always full. So, like I said, I'll check and call you later." Denise tried to turn and walk away but he grabbed a small piece of her jacket.

"I can't get a hug or a kiss? Something to tide me over until later," he pleaded.

The fact he stood there begging turned Denise off but she knew the only way she could get rid of Tyrone was to give him a hug. She reached up and then let go, but he tried to quickly kiss her lips. However, she quickly moved her head so he caught her cheek.

Thank God I have good reflexes.

"Bye Tyrone," Denise replied as they parted ways.

Lord, why do I keep talking to this fool? It has to be the sex. Denise exhaled as she turned around saw Tyrone get in his car and leave. He was like a bad virus, or better yet, a habit she couldn't seem to drop. Because, just when she thought she was free of him, he found a way to come right back into her life. She didn't know why she even tolerated him and his annoying antics but figured part of the reason why she continued to stick around him was because they were so sexually compatible. That man could handle his business in the bedroom like none other. His skills were the only variable in the entire equation that truly made sense, justifying the fact she hadn't cut him off.

The moment Denise hit the cardio area of the gym she spotted a fine, muscular man running on the treadmill next to her favorite elliptical machine. His muscles popped out of everywhere while his arms and legs had so much definition, she could tell at first glance he spent a lot of time working on his body. In all the times she had come to the gym, she never saw him so she used the opportunity to introduce herself.

"Excuse me, is anyone using this treadmill?" Denise asked the guy who ran toward the treadmill next to the one she wanted to use.

"No," the man replied and kept running.

She was surprised all the man said to her was "no." Usually, she had to fight them off with a stick. In any event, she put her headphones on and proceeded to warm up. After spending about twenty minutes on the elliptical, the sexy, muscle-bound guy spoke.

"It's hard to find a woman who's in shape," he stated as she kept on with her workout as if she didn't hear a word he said.

"Do you come here a lot?" he asked. She looked over at him with a blank expression on her face.

"Why do you want to know?"

"I just wondered. I'm a new trainer and I don't see many women come in here."

"What do you mean? All kinds of women work-out at this gym."

"Not any as fine as you." He looked her up and down as if she was a piece of meat. Denise decreased her levels, jumped off the machine, and picked up her towel.

"Is that all you have to say?" she quizzed.

"No. Actually, I just moved here from Detroit to be closer to family and I want make some new friends. Help ease my transition." He flashed a Hollywood smile.

31

For a second, Denise almost lost her composure but managed to remain cool. However, she couldn't deny the man was absolutely gorgeous - not to mention he had a body that would make LL Cool J want to hit up the gym more often.

"So, you expect me to be your friend?" Denise asked.

"Yes."

"How do you expect me to be your friend when I don't even know your name?"

"My name Darnell but my peoples call me D." He shook her hand.

"What's yours?"

"Marie," she replied, since she rarely gave out her real name when first meeting a guy. "If you'll excuse me, I have to get ready and go."

Denise walked away and went into the locker room. She called Randy to let him know she was on her way to the church, took a shower, and got dressed. As she exited, Denise saw Darnell in the lounge.

"Dang girl! I thought you'd never get dressed." He smiled. She smacked her lips.

"I didn't tell you to wait for me." She walked past him.

"Marie, why are you so mean? I thought we were friends now?"

"When did I ever say we were friends? Did I give you that impression?" She stood with her hands on her hips.

"You treat everybody like this?" he asked as she took her keys out of her purse.

"Look, I'm really late and need to be going. So, if you're still interested in being my friend, give me your number. Maybe, I'll give you a call or something." Denise zipped up her black leather jacket as he scribbled his number on a piece of paper and handed it to her.

"Like I said, I'll think about giving you a call," Denise replied and moved away from Darnell with his number in her hand and a smile on her face. She walked the entire distance to her car and could feel Darnell's eyes stuck to her behind like a logo. She knew he was definitely feeling her but she didn't want him to know she felt the same way just yet. Yes, he was sexy. However, she just met him and wanted to see where he was coming from first before she made any serious moves.

In her car, Denise put in Janet Jackson's 20 year old CD and let the softness of her voice help her unwind as she drove toward the church. She managed to push herself a little too hard while working out and it was slowly but surely catching up to her. Her back muscles tightened on her and she wished she used the extra time after her workout to stretch rather than chit chat with Darnell. She had to admit, he was cute though and figured she would call him in due time. However, the phone rang so she answered as she saw her beloved Jackson's name on the display.

"Hey, baby! Just the woman I wanna talk to," he said.

"Just the man I wanna talk to," she replied as she smiled from ear to ear as Jackson had that type of effect on her. "I just finished at the gym. What you doing?"

"Been in court all day but thinking of you, nonetheless. That's why I'm calling."

"Jackson, that's so sweet of you."

"I enjoyed our time together. I wished I could've stayed longer."

"I wish you could've stayed too. The time you spent in town just wasn't long enough." Denise's heart beat picked up its pace while thinking about their brunch date.

"So, I wasn't just calling to hear your beautiful voice. Wanted you to know I sent you a little something by the way of Western Union to say thank you."

"Ah. You didn't have to."

"I know, but I wanted to. Look, I have to go, but, it's there. You can pick it up."

33

"You're too much."

"We'll talk soon," he responded. After she ended her call, she made a quick detour toward Wal-mart. And while in their customer service line, Randy called.

"Are you still coming to have lunch with me?" he asked upon her answering.

"I'm on my way, honey." Denise spoke in a quick manner since the lady in front of her was cussing the cashier out, causing all kinds of unnecessary commotion. Denise tried to focus on talking to her husband but, with the woman practically losing her mind, she found concentrating to be difficult.

"Where are you, Denise? It sounds like a lot of noise in the background."

"Oh. I stopped by Wal-mart on my way to you."

"What are you getting at Wal-mart? It's on the other side of town."

"I forgot to buy some detergent when I was here the other day so I wanted to pick up some while I thought about it."

"Alright. Well, I'll wait until to you get here to order our food."

"Okay, I'll see you in twenty minutes."

Denise hung up with Randy just as the head cashier asked her, "Can I help you?"

The woman instructed Denise to fill out a form so she could claim her money. Denise smiled as she wrote down the necessary information. She couldn't believe Jackson decided to send her more money even though he had given her some when he was in town. She concluded he must've really missed her to shell out that kind of cash but, in the same breath, Jackson was that kind of man. He was like that since the first day they met, which was one of the reasons why Denise made sure he stayed around.

The cashier counted out ten one hundred dollar bills and handed them to her. "You have a nice day," she said.

"I sure will," Denise replied.

As she walked to her car she couldn't contain her happiness. From day one, Jackson said he would always take care of her and had kept his word. Before she put the key in the ignition, she pulled out her wad of money. She wanted to count it again before she pulled off. She loved money. She loved the way it felt in her hands. She loved the way it smelled, especially brand new money. She flipped through the small stack and smiled as she put it back into her purse. The one thing she loved more than sex was definitely money. Of course, she loved God and her husband but nothing made her more excited than those two powerful words: money and sex. When she saw her phone vibrating again, she didn't care to answer. She knew it could only be one person.

"What do you want, Tyrone? Didn't we just talk?" Denise screamed into the phone as a way of saying hello to the growing pain in her side.

"Hold up. Why are you in a bad mood? I just called to see if you still coming over later on," he responded.

"I said I was going to call you back, not the other way around."

"I thought you forgot and wanted to catch you before you got too busy," he continued. Denise's phone line beeped and she knew she had to answer it.

"Hold on, my line is clicking." She took the phone away from her ear and pressed the green button then saw her husband's name pop up on the screen.

"Hello baby. How far are you from the church?" Randy asked.

"About ten minutes. Why?"

"Denise, I'm so sorry, but I have to cancel our lunch."

"Why?"

"I forgot I have a meeting with a few of the ministers. It's about an upcoming event and has to be taken care of today."

"Randy, the meeting can't wait until after our lunch?"

"I'm afraid not, sweetie. I'm really sorry but I promise I'll make it up to you somehow."

"Well, how about we plan on going out to dinner?"

Randy sighed. "I'm afraid I can't. Have a few people I need to counsel before I come home so I won't be there until late. I really apologize for doing this to you."

"Whatever Randy. So, I guess I'll see you later." Denise pressed the end button, not allowing Randy a chance to respond because that wasn't the first time something like this happened. There had been many times she planned to do things with him and he canceled because of church business. She tried to be understanding as best as she could but, over the years, it felt like she always played second to his ministry. That's why, when she did go out and do her own thing, she felt well within her right to do so. *It's fine, Randy. If you don't have any time to spend with me today, I know someone who does.*

Denise tried to switch the phone line to tell Tyrone she was free to meet up with him but he had hung up. So, she decided to send Mr. Bug-a-Boo himself a message to let him know she was on her way over. She knew he was livid about being on hold for so long, but would be happy to see the message that read:

Hey Sweetie. Still wanna get together this evening? I can't wait to see you.

In less than a minute and a half he responded by saying he couldn't wait to see her too. She smiled as she placed her phone on the seat and paid attention to the road.

I got this dude wrapped around my little finger and I love it. It's a great feeling to know someone will do whatever I want them to do when I want them to. Randy may have canceled our plans, but I got some of my own tonight and they don't include him.

Denise pulled up in his driveway in less than twenty five minutes and saw Tyrone's midnight blue Acura RL sitting in the middle of the driveway. She walked up to the door and tried the handle to see if it was locked but, to her surprise, it wasn't so she opened it. As she walked closer to his dining room, she saw him with his back turned and talking on his speaker phone. She didn't bother to alert him of her presence since she wanted to hear what he spoke about.

"What happened at work that caused you leave me that voicemail," Tyrone said.

"Yo, I met me someone today," a male voiced responded.

"For real? That's cool. Where did you meet her?"

"At work, and she's beautiful man. Think she might be a keeper, for real."

"You feel like that already? You just met her. Is it that serious?"

"Na'll man, it's just something about her. I don't know what it is, but I have got to make her mine," the voice continued.

"Did you get her number?"

"Come on, man. You know I got that. But, I can't wait for her to call me."

Tyrone sucked his teeth and let out a chuckle. "Thought you just said you got her number. Why you waiting on her?"

"Meant to say, can't wait for us to talk. It just came out the wrong way, that's all."

"Whatever you say, but I know exactly what you meant." Tyrone laughed and turned around to find Denise standing there, listening closely to every word he said.

"Yo! My lady just got here. I'll call you back later." Tyrone ended the conversation with not as much as a second thought.

"You didn't have to stop because of me. I was actually enjoying it." She smiled, walked up to him, and kissed his lips.

"It's cool. Just talking to one of my cousins. He just moved in town and called to tell me 'bout this woman he met today."

"I heard all that," she replied.

Tyrone took Denise's purse and placed it down on his table, then took her jacket off for her. Slowly, he planted kisses on the back of her neck and started to remove her clothing at the same time.

"That's enough talk about him."

Now, she thought they would at least grab some dinner before doing anything but he had other plans. As Tyrone lifted her up by her waist and slid her body onto the table, Denise realized she was, in fact, the main course that evening and it was perfectly fine with her. With the way he touched and kissed her body, she lost all train of thought. Tyrone affected on her in that kind of way and it was to a point that, when they were together, she would even forget the date. Earlier that day, he had managed to get on her last nerve but had been wonderful at making up.

Chapter Three

Denise woke up the next morning exhausted, thinking about how Tyrone worked her over the previous night. When she got home, all she could do was collapse on the bed. She thanked God for taking a shower at his place otherwise she wouldn't have taken one at all. Randy still wasn't home by the time she arrived which wasn't a surprise to her because, as the senior pastor of the largest church in Youngstown, he always put in extremely long hours. So, groggily, she got up and went down to the kitchen to make breakfast. And, by the time she cooked up the eggs, Randy came down the steps.

"Whatever you're making down here smells really good. It woke me up." He came behind Denise and wrapped his arms around her. He stood there for a moment and inhaled her scent, loving the way she smelled.

"I made you an omelet," Denise answered, not even responding to the affection he showed, acting as if she was still mad about the canceled lunch date.

"Thanks, baby. I know it's gonna be good." He reached around and tried to kiss Denise on her cheek but could tell she was upset by her facial expression and her body language.

"Are you still upset about yesterday?"

"Kind of... I feel like every time we plan something it's always canceled because of something at the church. I know you're a busy man with a lot of responsibility but, remember, you're my husband first," Denise replied and put their omelets onto plates.

"Denise, I am so sorry. I've been doing that a lot and really do apologize from the bottom of my heart. I promise I'll do better. I hope you forgive me," Randy said with a sincere look on his face.

"I forgive you," Denise answered and kissed him. She understood that Randy had to balance a lot on his plate but she always seemed to feel that she was on the back burner.

"Since you're not mad at me anymore, can you do me a huge favor today?"

"What do you need me to do?"

"Stop by my parents' house and see how they're doing?" Randy asked.

"You want me to go over and see how your parents are doing?"

"Yes. Go see if they need anything. My mother called and said dad has been a little under the weather lately."

"You sure you want me to go?"

"Don't worry, babe. Everything's going to be okay. I know what you're trying to get at."

"Now, I don't have a problem with going over there and checking on them, but you know how your mom is," Denise replied. Randy didn't answer. Instead, he gave her the "look." The one he always gave her before they went over his parent's house, where she already knew what he would say before he said it. "Randy, I promise. I'll try and get along with your mother," she said before he even opened his mouth.

"Thank you. I really appreciate you doing this for me."

"You're welcome. Anything for you," she replied but, at the same time, thought about how much Randy would owe her. Asking her to go and check on his parents was almost like requesting she go to the freeway and play in the middle of traffic, as she always had problems with his mother, Alice.

I promise to try and get along with her, but if she says something out of the way to me like she always does, it's broke. It's all up to her. If she wants to start something with me then I will have no choice but to do what I have to do.

After Denise finished eating with Randy, she went upstairs and put on one of her least form-fitting outfits. Randy's mother always seemed to have issues with Denise's clothing choices so she was very careful about what she wore around her. She settled on a pair of plain True Religion jeans and a white blouse. While her outfit wasn't extremely fashionable, it was still cute and would suffice for time being.

As she drove across town to visit her in-laws, Denise said a silent prayer. *Lord, please help me. And please let his mother not say anything out of the way to me because if she does I don't know what I will do. In Jesus name. Amen.*

When Denise pulled into the driveway of his parents' three bedroom, split-level home, she didn't see their black Buick Century parked in the driveway and didn't think anything of it because they usually parked in the garage.

She knocked on the door for about ten minutes and was just about to leave when her father-in-law, Randy Sr., came to the door. The only reason why she hadn't left was because she could hear someone walking around.

"What brings you over our way, baby girl?" he said while opening the front door and seeing her standing on the front stoop. He reached out and gave her a hug.

"Hey Daddy Tate. I thought I'd stop over and check to see how you're doing. For a minute, I didn't think anyone was home. I've been out here for a while."

"I'm sorry we left you standing out there so long. I was in the study reading my Bible. Not sure where Alice at."

As Denise walked into the house and saw her mother-in-law sitting on the couch flipping through an *Ebony* magazine, she realized Alice was the person she heard walking around.

"I'm sorry, Denise. Were you at the front door? I didn't even hear you." Alice blinked her eyes then plastered the fakest smile she could on her face.

Denise knew she probably saw her pull up to the house and decided to leave her standing outside looking stupid. Denise also knew she did whatever she could to push her to the limit and was determined to not allow that happen. Alice always found a way to push Denise's buttons just to watch her lose her cool. Then, that way, she would have something to run and tell her son about.

"Yes, Mama Tate, I was at the door," Denise said between clenched teeth. *I told Randy I would be nice. But, if that heifer says or does anything else out of line, it's on and poppin' for real. It's only so much I can take.* Denise sat down next to her father-in-law and put her Gucci purse on the coffee table.

"I'm so sorry, honey. Please forgive me," Alice replied, but Denise knew the only reason she mustered up the apology was because Randy Sr. would've brought it to her attention if she didn't.

"Baby, the next time you come over, please use your key. That's why we gave you one," said Daddy Tate. Denise smiled as Alice shot her an evil look like you better not ever use that key to come up in my house. Denise used her key many times before until Alice complained to Randy about it. Ever since Denise knew Alice had a problem with her using it, she decided not to use it at all.

"I'll use my key next time," Denise added, which made Alice roll her eyes. Denise cracked a smile, knowing she could irritate Alice.

"So, how's my favorite daughter- in-law in the whole wide world?" he asked.

"Dad, I'm your only daughter-in-law." She laughed.

"Oh, that is right."

"You're so silly," she continued.

Daddy Tate tried to make light of the conversation which always brightened Denise's day. He was fully aware that his wife didn't particularly care for Denise, but that didn't influence how he felt about her. He considered Denise to be his own daughter and was glad his son married her. But, Alice had a different point of view. She didn't trust Denise and probably never would.

"So, what you been up to, dad?" Denise asked.

"Haven't been doing too much of anything. Been fooling round in the garden picking up weeds, trimming the bushes out front, and I've been going over my study notes for the sermon I'm preaching next week at Mt. Olive."

"Sounds to me like you've been busy," Denise replied, but Alice cut in and didn't give him a chance to speak.

"Too busy and know he needs to slow down. His doctor told him." Alice looked up from her magazine and rolled her eyes at him.

"I know what my doctor said," he retorted.

"What did he say, dad?"

"All I need to do is incorporate more rest into my schedule because I'm putting extra stress on my heart by doing so much."

"Are you listening?" Denise asked then waited to see what he was going to say.

"I'm resting right now, see." He put his feet up on the coffee table and leaned back like he was taking a nap then chuckled as Denise shook her head.

"Daddy Tate, please do me a favor and make sure you're listening to what the doctor says. I don't want you to get sick," she stated.

"Denise, don't worry about me. I'll be fine. So, what you been up to, my darling?"

"You know me. Just trying to be the best first lady I can, besides trying to convince your son to slow down a little bit because he works so hard too."

"Well honey, you're doing the right thing by trying to get Randy to rest because he'll run himself ragged trying to keep up with everybody. And, believe me, I've been there and done that. It gets real old after a while," said Daddy Tate.

"Well, the church can't run by itself. Somebody has to do it and the best man for the job is my son," Alice interjected.

"I know. But, let's be honest. He can't be everything to everybody. Sometimes the church acts like he is Jesus and, if he's not there, they are going to die." Denise looked over at her mother-in-law to make sure she listened to every word she said.

"You're right, sweetheart. I know exactly what you're saying. My church used to try and do the same thing to me. But, you know what I keep tellin' him he has to do sometimes?"

"What is that?" Denise asked.

"He needs to learn to say no. That church will run just fine if he takes off a couple off days to rest. That's the same stuff they tried to do to me. Don't you remember, Alice?"

Alice didn't respond. Instead, she got an attitude with her husband. She was tired of him always taking Denise's side when she was around as if he tried extra hard to please her. She couldn't stand Denise and figured there was no need in pretending.

"I remember. But, I also remember how Second Street Baptist operated so smooth when you were actively running the church," Alice replied as she rolled her eyes and crossed her arms.

Denise grew sick and tired of her rolling her eyes.

Randy Sr. ignored his wife and turned to face Denise. "Well, baby, don't worry. You're doing a good job with trying to get my son to slow down and delegate some of his responsibility. He may not understand why you're doing it now but I guarantee he'll thank you later."

Alice picked her *Ebony* back up and continued flipping through the pages. She didn't care to carry on any more conversation with Denise. As far as she knew, Denise probably only came over there to visit her husband anyway. She lifted her head over the magazine and watched how Denise carried on with him. She observed how Denise got all giggly and flirty when she approached him and Mama Tate didn't like it not one bit. Honestly, it wasn't that she didn't trust her husband because she knew he would never cheat on her. But, she surely didn't trust Denise. There was something about her that proceeded to creep and crawl underneath Alice's skin and she couldn't figure out what it was about Denise that disturbed her. She couldn't quite put her finger on it. But, she knew one day, if there was something to be revealed, that God would definitely expose it. Alice just prayed that she would be able to take a front seat when it actually did.

After about twenty-five minutes, Denise rose. "I'm about to get out of here because I have some errands to run, but if you need anything just give me a call," Denise replied as she picked up her purse from the coffee table. Randy Sr. stood and gave her a hug. Alice slapped her magazine down so hard on the table that the sound caused them to both look in her direction.

"Thanks Denise. And, thanks for stopping by, honey," Daddy Tate replied as he walked her to the door. Denise didn't even attempt to hug Alice. She wouldn't even bother to get close to her because, with the way

Alice looked at her, she would probably try to put her in a headlock and choke the life out of her.

"Goodbye Mama," Denise replied as she walked out the door, knowing Alice couldn't stand when she referenced her that way but she didn't care. She saw it as pure satisfaction.

Denise left their house and drove to Austintown to buy some hair products. On the way there, she passed by the tiny, closed down storefront that used to be their former church home. She looked at the front of the building which was boarded up with thick wood and her mind flooded with memories. Her thoughts concentrated and focused on how life for her and Randy was in the not so distant past.

God brought them a mighty long way. She went from living in a overly populated, middle-class neighborhood to a custom built home in Canfield Township, which was an area where most African Americans couldn't even afford to drive through. But Denise didn't feel out of place among all her white neighbors. Instead, she felt like it was where she was supposed to live from the beginning. As she continued to drive, her mind took her back to when they first got married and Randy promised to give her everything she ever wanted, that she wouldn't have to work because he would make everything possible.

But, in the beginning, he was just starting out as the assistant pastor of a very small church on the west side of town and wasn't making much money. In fact, Randy had to take a part-time job at Wal-Mart just to make ends meet. With the combination of both incomes, he was able to buy a two bedroom house on the north side. During their first couple of years as newlyweds, Denise couldn't believe how Randy had her living. He promised her the world and that's what she expected. So, she felt like he had not delivered. She thought she deserved the finer things in life and, if he wasn't capable of affording them, she would find someone who could.

She didn't like him being the assistant at that church because it seemed to drain their bank account rather than add to it. She remembered how many times the church couldn't pay him. And Randy being a true saint and man of God, he simply accepted it because his Lord would take care of him. But, like Job's wife, Denise couldn't have disagreed more.

She understood the Christian thought but also knew it didn't pay the electricity, gas, water, or cable companies. She constantly encouraged him to find a position in another church, preferably a bigger one, but Randy searched high and low for almost two years and hadn't had any luck in finding a better position.

After struggling and trying to hang in there with Randy, she decided she had enough. Denise was ready to be done with him and had actually planned to be with Jackson until Randy received a phone call changed everything. She sat at the kitchen table sipping on orange juice and eating a bowl of oatmeal while he was on the phone. She couldn't figure out who he was talking to but, whoever it was, they surely had his full and undivided attention because he was completely zoned out and engrossed in this conversation.

"Yes. I can meet you there today. Thank you so much." Randy placed the phone back on the receiver.

"Who was it? And, why are you looking like that?" Denise studied her husband's face as he sat down at the table across from her but said nothing. She began to get worried when he didn't answer then he grabbed her hands and spoke.

"That was Pastor Keith Jones."

"Pastor Keith Jones? Wait a minute. Senior pastor at Oakdale Baptist Church?"

"You remember him," he continued but Denise thoughts had already moved on.

Oh, how could I forget? He has the biggest African-American church in the city. He's also one of the

47

finest men I ever met. Tall, chocolate complexion and a pair of gray eyes to make you think about committing a couple of sins.

"Well, what he say?" Denise attempted to camouflage the smile trying to creep up on her face.

"He and wife have accepted a position to co-pastor a church in Florida."

"Is that it? Why would he just call and tell you that? He could've sent you a post card for all that."

"Just hold on, babe. He wants to meet with me about possibly being his replacement." Randy smiled. Denise leaned forward and tried to process what her husband had just told her.

"Did you just say he wants you to be the next pastor of Oakdale?"

"Before you get excited, he said he is considering me, which means I am not the only one he's thinking about for the position. I still have to meet with him personally so I don't have it just yet."

"When is this meeting?"

"Later on tonight at The Springfield Grille. For dinner."

"Well, call me and let me know what time you want me to be back and ready," she said. Denise got up from the table and put on her white K-Swiss sneakers.

"Where are you going?"

"I'm going out. There are some things I have to do to make sure tonight is perfect."

Denise remembered how she made a few quick trips around town to pick up outfits for both of them to wear. Denise figured the clothes they owned weren't suitable enough and, if he was going to land the job, they had to look the part. She decided to buy Randy a navy and sky blue Stacy Adams suit from Remo's Menswear and she picked up a matching church suit from Macy's. By the time her last minute shopping spree ended, she had maxed out two major credit cards. She knew Randy would be mad at her for making those purchases, but she looked at

48

as an investment. She must've had some type of ability to see into the future because, by the end of dinner, the pastor offered Randy the position.

However, when Randy heard the offer, he said he would have to pray about it. Denise had to catch herself from rolling her eyes too hard at him. She couldn't believe he didn't say yes right way. She figured he should've been itching to, especially since it was Lord's work. Even though Randy delayed answering, she knew he would eventually say yes. There were too many perks to turn it down.

First off, Randy would receive a six figure salary with a fifteen thousand dollar bonus and a brand new car. He would also have a top of the line office with a one bedroom apartment directly connected to it. When Denise thought about all benefits, it made her want to become a minister so she could take the position herself. She didn't understand what on earth Randy had to think about. As far as she was concerned, her mind was made up. That position was created for her husband. She knew he always desired to be the pastor of a large congregation one day. So, for him, it was a dream come true. When she considered the rewards she would receive as first lady, she reasoned within herself it was the type of life she was supposed to live.

Like anticipated, Randy accepted the position. And, shortly thereafter, Denise upgraded her lifestyle. She no longer bought clothes from Wal-Mart, Target, and Sears. She filled her closet with expensive designer items from all the finest boutiques. Randy didn't have a problem with Denise's lavish spending habits. He wanted her to have the best. So, if having the latest outfit was what she wanted, she got it. In fact, the minute he started to see serious money growing in the bank account, he hired a contractor to design her dream home. He remembered how she would go on and on about how she wanted it to look and what she wanted in it. Those were the things he made sure he was included.

Eighteen months later, the ultimate luxury home suitable enough for his queen was finished. And once she saw it before her eyes, she was so glad she wasn't stupid enough to leave him. She had already stuck it out for almost a decade when he didn't have a dime, so she figured it would be absolute foolish to leave at that point because all of his money was rightfully hers.

Denise's mind started to forget about their humble beginning as she pulled up into the subdivision located in an exclusive neighborhood. She parked her Benz in the center of her driveway and pressed the button on her car alarm. Then, she looked around at all she had been blessed with and a huge smile crept across her face. She thought about how fabulous her life and how she wouldn't trade it for the world.

Chapter Four

Denise sat in the living room painting her nails when she decided to call Tyrone. And, while waiting on her polish to dry, she put him on speaker phone. For a while, the line just rang and she thought it would go to his voicemail until he eventually picked up.

"I'm surprised to hear from you. It's been like two weeks," he said.

"Tyrone, don't even start with me, you know how busy my life can get sometimes." Denise tried her best to have a light, drama free conversation with him but she knew that wasn't possible.

"Yeah, I know how busy your life can be, Little Miss Preacher's Wife. How can I ever forget?" He chuckled to himself.

"It sounds to me like someone's mad," Denise said as she began to fan her nails.

"Well, let's see. Every time I think we're going to be able to spend some time together, you always find a way to conveniently cancel. Who wouldn't be mad?"

"You are over exaggerating. That happened like once or twice, months ago."

"It don't matter. We still don't spend any time together. You know it."

She couldn't argue with him because they hadn't been spending much time together but, after all, she was married. She didn't understand how he could just expect her to drop everything to be at his beck and call. That wasn't going to happen and he should've known but insisted on pushing the envelope as far as he could.

"So, why haven't we seen each other in a few weeks?" Tyrone asked.

"Been busy. We just had a conference and that took up all my time."

"So, let me ask you this. What have you got planned this evening?"

"Nothing. You trying to see me or are you still upset?"

"What time you coming over," Tyrone replied.

"How about seven?" Denise offered, knowing that if he called himself being angry at her then he wouldn't be for long.

"Seven it is. Denise, don't cancel." Tyrone hung up the phone yet she didn't know what he meant by his last statement. He must've thought he put his foot down but Denise wasn't scared of him to say the least. Then, no sooner than they hung up, she was right back on her phone dialing Terri's number.

"This is Terri. How can I help you?"

"What's up, Miss Big Shot Attorney?"

"Hey Denise. What's going on?" Terri said in her more relaxed, natural voice.

"Nothing. Just wondering what you were doing tonight."

"Actually, I've been working like crazy. Trying to finish up this one case so I probably won't be going anywhere."

"Go ahead and make that money. But, I called to see if you'll do me a huge favor."

"Anything for my best friend."

"I have other plans after Bible study and was wondering if you could cover for me. I'ma tell Randy I'm stopping by your house so we could catch up."

"What kind of plans do you have?"

"Plans."

"Oh, I see. You have man plans. How do you do it?"

"Do what?" Denise asked.

"How do you manage to stay married and do your own thing on the side? I'm single and sometimes I can't hold it all together."

"I don't know. I must have a special ability or something." Denise laughed.

"Well, if I'm covering for you. Can I least know who you gone be with?"

"If you must, Tyrone."

"You still talking to him?"

"Why you say it like that?"

"I don't know what you see in him."

"You know what? Sometimes, I don't know what I see in him either until we hit the bedroom. And then, I know exactly what it is. The brotha' definitely got skills."

"Whatever you say. I pray and ask God to bless me with one and he turns around and gives you two. I just don't understand because, if I were you, Randy would be all I need."

"He is. But, sometimes a sista needs Tyrone or Jackson."

"Whatever you say. But, you know I can only cover for you for so long."

"I know but don't worry about it. I got everything under control." Denise really had no intentions of changing how she lived her life. She was amazed at the fact she could go out and have her fun yet still remain married to Randy. With him being busy, he never seemed to notice how frequently she was absent.

"You know you owe me big time," Terri said.

"I owe you a whole lot. If it wasn't for you I don't know where I would be sometimes."

"It's cool. That's what friends do."

"You got that right."

"Well, I have to get off of this phone. But, please make sure you call me later so you can fill me in on all of the juicy details."

"You know I will." Denise had a devilish smirk on her face as she hung up the phone with her best friend.

She loved Randy with all her heart and had actually considered giving up her other men to be the faithful wife but justified her actions by reasoning that they didn't have anything to do with him and what he didn't know wouldn't hurt him. She had desires that needed to be fulfilled and, whether it was Randy or some other man, she made sure all of them were met.

Denise thought back to the time when she was actually the good wife she only appeared to be. When they first decided to get married, she made a promise to herself that she wouldn't do anything to jeopardize her marital vows. Her father's affair made her realize marriage was way too sacred to mess it up by cheating, so she tried to do all she could in order to remain true. Even though temptation constantly came her way, she remained a virgin until she walked down the aisle. She'd taken pride in the fact she saved herself for the man she truly loved and was glad to be the one to present him with that gift. Denise knew that being twenty years old and keeping her virginity made a statement, but it was more of a personal one. By keeping herself out of sexual sin, she proved to herself she was not her father.

In the beginning of their marriage, Denise was so in love with the idea of matrimony and she enjoyed being married to Randy. He promised her the world and didn't want her to work at all. He told her he would provide everything and she literally hung onto every word he said. She believed he would give her everything she'd ever dreamed of and, when that failed to happen, he started to make her feel the same way her father made her feel - disappointed. She began to not trust in everything Randy said anymore. She even started to sink into a deep depression because she felt like he was beginning to let her down just like her father did years ago. And to feel disappointment took her back to the feelings she experienced in her childhood so she began to grow restless in her marriage.

The contentment and satisfaction she once found solely in Randy wasn't sufficient enough to sustain her. She wanted more. So, after a couple of weeks trying to lift her best friend's spirit, Terri suggested Denise go out with some of the people from the law office where she worked as a legal secretary. Denise attempted to decline the offer, but Terri wouldn't take no for an answer so reluctantly she agreed.

"Terri, I'm going to feel so out of place when we go out tonight."

"Shut up Denise. I don't want to hear it. Now, you've been moping around and being depressed for weeks, so you're coming out with me tonight. Besides, you act like we're going to the club. We're only going to Jillian's."

"I know. I'm just saying I haven't been out since I've been married."

"That's my point. You need to go out tonight. And I promise you, you're gonna have fun, Miss Thing."

So, since her best friend wasn't going to let her back out at the last minute, she had to go out. When they arrived at Jillian's, the entire staff from the law office where Terri worked was there, including a couple of new faces. So, Terri made sure she was properly introduced.

"This is Andrea, Gabrielle, and Jackson," she said. Denise went down the line and spoke to everyone. When she got to Jackson, he decided to take her hand and kiss it.

"Nice to meet you, Denise." He smiled. Denise became mesmerized by his pearly whites and appearance.

She knew by the gray on his head that he was older but he really didn't look like it. He was absolutely one hundred percent fine and there was no denying upon first glance that Denise was attracted to him. She was kind of caught off guard that he chose to kiss her hand instead of say hello like everyone else but figured he was just trying to be nice. Throughout dinner, she found Jackson staring across the table from her and sneaking glances every second he got. Then, he occasionally tried to strike up conversation when he could. At times, she could barely concentrate on what anyone else was saying because all she could do was admire him. Denise paid attention to the way he walked, the conversation he carried and, most of all, the wad of bills he kept flashing. By the time they walked over to the bowling alley, they were in deep conversation. Terri took notice to what was going on and decided to pull her to the side.

"It looks like you're really enjoying yourself."

"I am."

"I see. You better be careful about Jackson because it looks like he trying to talk to you."

"You're silly. I don't see where he's trying to do that. We're just holding a conversation. That's all."

"Denise, you can try to play dumb all you want but I know how Jackson is. He's not going be satisfied until he has you in his bed. Trust me."

"This is all harmless. Besides, he knows I'm married."

"Believe me. He doesn't care."

Terri must've known Jackson like the back of her hand because, before the end of the night, they exchanged cell numbers. Then, that next week, he managed to invite Denise over to his place for dinner. When he had initially asked her she turned him down, mainly because she was married and didn't think it was appropriate to be having dinner with another man. But, Jackson explained that he respected her marriage and would never try to come between them. He said they would get together to simply have dinner and nothing more. So, Denise agreed to just have dinner.

When Randy asked her where she was going, she told him she out with Terri to Cleveland. But, in actuality, she went twenty minutes across town to where Jackson rented a loft. For a minute, she thought Randy would become suspicious and ask why when they had just gone the week before but he didn't question her so she took that as her cue to enjoy herself for the evening. When Denise pulled up to his loft that sat at the edge of Millcreek Park, she checked her appearance in the mirror.

Denise rang his doorbell and, to her surprise, he answered the door immediately.

"You look amazing," Jackson said as he took her coat off and placed it on his coat rack. Denise decided to wear a jean skirt that touched the middle of her thigh, a black scoop neck sweater hanging slightly off her shoulders, with a pair of black stilettos.

"Thanks. You don't look so bad yourself. You have a nice place here."

"Thank you. You're more than welcome to take a look around if you want." Denise removed her black satin stilettos and walked around his lavish bachelor pad. As her feet sank into the plush cream carpet covering his entire apartment floor, she began to feel relaxed and comfortable in his space. She walked in and out of each room and she was very impressed.

"Where did you learn to decorate like this? It's beautiful."

"Thank you. I learned all of this from my mother. She's an interior designer."

"She definitely taught you well." Denise walked into the kitchen where he had dinner set up with candles. She went up to the stove and peeked into the pots. "And, you can cook, too?"

Jackson didn't answer instead he dimmed the lights and put on some slow jams. By the time Denise turned around, he stood right in front of her. "Can we dance?" He held out his hand and waited for her to accept but she walked away.

"Come on. Just one." He smiled at her hesitation, knowing she was reluctant. But, he also knew she was just as attracted to him as he was to her.

And, when Denise saw that million-dollar smile before her, she couldn't say no. Besides, she figured she would share one dance with him and that was all.

It's one harmless, little, slow dance. Besides, it's not like I'm kissing or having sex with him.

Jackson pulled Denise into his body and caressed her as they slow danced. Other than Randy, she had never been that close to another man. She thought it would be awkward but it felt good to have a fine, well-dressed, rich attorney hold her like they had known each other for years. He pulled her so tight that there wasn't any room in between them and she could even feel his heartbeat. As the slow jams played through his stereo, they danced to several songs. Denise just closed her eyes, inhaled his cologne, and became caught up in the moment. She had never felt that way about anyone except Randy and to feel that way about someone who she didn't know, scared her. Then, Jackson leaned in closer and kissed Denise on her lips.

"What was that for?" Denise snapped out of her daydream and looked at him.

"I'm sorry. I apologize, but it just seemed that you were feeling me like that."

"Oh, so you just gone kiss me without warning? You know I'm married." Denise crossed her arms. She couldn't believe he had the nerve to assume she even wanted to kiss him. He was an absolute dime piece but she wasn't going to let him know.

"I know you're married but that didn't stop you from coming over here."

"No it didn't. But I just came to have dinner. That's all."

"So you're going to sit here and tell me you are not attracted to me?"

"Nope," Denise answered real quickly.

"I think you're lying. Look me in my eyes and tell me you're not feeling me," he continued. Denise attempted but, for some reason, her mouth froze and she was unable to speak. Then, without warning again, he moved in and tasted her lips once more. But that time, she didn't stop him. She allowed herself to become involved and their kissing quickly turned to exploring each other's bodies with their hands. Before they knew it, they ended up on Jackson's room. He laid Denise down on his king size bed and began to plant small kisses from her mouth then made his way downward. Denise moaned in extreme pleasure as he began to satisfy something deep inside of her, something she never knew existed while it awakened a desire in her. Sex with him was spontaneous, spur of the moment, exciting and, most of all, extremely good.

After they performed for about an hour, she lay on one side of the bed and stared up at the ceiling. *I can't believe what I just did. Never in a million years would I have ever thought I would be lying up in a bed with someone other than my husband. I promised myself I would never cheat on my husband and now I've done it effortlessly.*

"Are you okay?" Jackson got up from bed and looked at Denise's puzzling facial expression.

"I'm fine."

"Are you sure because you don't look fine. I mean, you are fine but you look like something is wrong."

"No. I'm okay, really."

"Well, I'm going to heat up our food so we can finally eat dinner. I ran you a bath. It's ready," he said as he left the bedroom.

Denise went into the bathroom and shut the door behind her. She ran water in the sink and splashed her face a couple of times. After she dried it off, she caught a glimpse of herself in the mirror. She began to shake her head at what went down. She couldn't believe it. Ever since her father destroyed their lives by his infidelity, she made a vow to never let that happen to her. But, as she studied her own features in the mirror, she noticed she looked just like the very person she despised and wondered if their souls were as similar. She couldn't take it anymore and walked away.

Chapter Five

Denise arrived at Tyrone's only to find his house completely dark so she couldn't understand why he requested her presence at seven and wasn't home. *This man complains about not seeing me for two weeks and he ain't here. Oh, hell no.*

She pulled out her phone and called him but he didn't answer. She found that unusual for a person who usually picks up before it rang once. She hung up and redialed but went straight to his voicemail. She stepped out of her car and started up the driveway before she noticed scattered rose petals leading up the walkway. *He knows I love roses*, she thought. Once she made it to the front door, she saw there was a single, long stem rose and a piece of paper taped to it. She removed the flower and read the note.

The door is unlocked. Come inside.

Denise opened it. As she stepped over the threshold, she discovered the petals continued and served as an indication to where Tyrone was located. She smiled and inhaled the scent of the beautiful flower she carried in her hand. Soft jazz music played in the background and vanilla candles burned. Denise walked through the living room, the kitchen, and into the dining area where the trail ended.

"I see you like to follow directions," Tyrone said as he got up from the table set up for a romantic dinner for two. He walked over and planted a soft kiss on her hand.

"As soon as I saw the roses, I had no choice but to follow the directions. You're really giving me the star treatment right now. I'm surprised."

"Why? I enjoy doing things like this for you," Tyrone commented.

"I could've sworn you were mad at me earlier. I was definitely not your favorite person a couple of hours ago."

"Don't mind me. You know how I get when I can't see you. That's just the effect you have on me." Tyrone moved in a little closer and grabbed onto Denise's waist.

She inhaled his Armani Mania cologne. She loved the way he smelled when he wore it and he usually made sure to do so when they were together. Denise pulled Tyrone in even closer while he moved his hands from resting on the small of her back to grabbing her behind.

"I see you wore that for me," he said as he looked her up and down checking out the Apple Bottom outfit.

"Only for you," Denise said as she pulled away from him to take a look at the meal he'd prepared. Denise turned her head back around and stared at Tyrone who seemed to be looking at her as if he was almost in a trance. She knew the jeans with the matching red top were the cause of Tyrone's sudden stupor. It hugged her body in all the right places and left very little to the imagination. That's the way she liked it. With her being the first lady, there weren't too many places she could wear an outfit like that and get away with it. However, she could always wear more suggestive clothing around Tyrone and know he would appreciate it. "Look at you. You really went all out. You made Swiss steaks, mashed potatoes, and grilled vegetables. You were serious about seeing me tonight. Weren't you?"

"Yeah. I'm serious. Tonight's a special night. I wanted you to know I was thinking about you," Tyrone said as he walked into the kitchen and back into the dining room with two champagne flutes.

"Thank you." Denise smiled while taking her glass and sitting down at the table as he pulled her chair out for her. Denise could smell the aroma from her plate and she couldn't wait to eat. But just as she picked up her fork to taste her food, Tyrone motioned for her to wait.

"Before we eat, I would like to toast," Tyrone announced as he cleared his throat.

"What are we toasting?" Denise asked.

"I know you keep hearing me say tonight is special. Well, this night is very significant to us. It's our one year anniversary."

"Our one year anniversary? Of what?" Denise asked with confusion on her face.

"Come on, Denise. We've been together a year now," he explained but she still looked puzzled.

Hold on. I know this man isn't counting the days and marking our anniversary like we were boyfriend and girlfriend. He must be insane. "Tyrone, I thought that we agreed not to keep track of how long we've been seeing each other. You know how I feel about that." Denise sat her glass down on the table and stood up.

"I know but I wanted to... no harm right?" Tyrone said as he rose up.

"I can't believe you. You know what we agreed upon! And time after time, you insist on doing your own thing."

"Wait one second. I know what we talked about in the beginning. But as time went on, things changed. Plus, you told me we're going to be together and that's what I'm holding on to. The problem is I don't know how much longer I can wait."

"And what's that supposed to mean?"

"I love you. I really want to be with you. It's hard seeing you married to someone else. The way I feel about you, you should be with me. Not him. And it just makes me crazy."

Denise took it as her cue to leave. She started walking toward the front door so she could get out of there because she couldn't stand when he got all deep and emotional.

"You're not going to say nothing. You're just going to leave?" Tyrone asked as he hurried behind her and shut the front door right before she opened it.

"Yes, I'm leaving. I don't have anything else to say."

"Are you mad?" Tyrone asked.

"What do you think? I really don't appreciate this right now and I'm out." Denise attempted to walk out the door again and Tyrone placed his hand on it.

"Denise, please don't go."

"Move your hand, Tyrone. I'm leaving," she stated. Tyrone moved but grabbed her hand and held onto it.

"Look, I'm sorry about tonight. I just got a little carried away that's all. I really didn't mean to make you mad. Don't leave...stay," Tyrone pleaded.

For a moment, Tyrone didn't know how his words influenced her but he hoped she would decide to remain. While he stood there holding her waist, she still seemed as if she wasn't affected by what he said. But, just when he thought she was going to move away, she allowed him to pull her closer and shut the front door again.

"Give me a chance to show you how much I've missed you," he whispered.

Denise wanted to walk out the door but it was something about Tyrone that seemed almost as strong as a gravitational force she was too weak to fight. No matter what she tried to do, she always found herself coming back.

She appeared as if she couldn't bear to be around him sometimes but, truthfully, Denise really did care about Tyrone. He did things to irritate her; however, she appreciated how he took time out of his schedule to make her feel special. He always put her first in all he did and Denise took notice. Giving Denise his undivided attention was one of the very things that kept him in the picture.

"Do you know that no matter how hard I try I cannot stay mad at you?" Denise said as she traced his chest with her fingers.

"I know," he replied.

"How you figure?" she asked.

"Because if you were still mad, you wouldn't be laying up in my bed with me," he continued but Denise slapped him on his arm.

"Shut up." She shook her head.

"I'm serious," Tyrone said.

"I know. You are… nasty."

"That's how you like me." He smiled and then kissed her.

Denise's cell phone began to ring.

"Hold up. Let me get that," she said as she stopped him in mid-kiss then ran to answer it. She knew it was Randy by the ring tone.

"Hello," Denise said after putting the phone up to her ear.

"Where you at?" Randy asked and her eyes almost popped out of their sockets.

"Hey babe, I didn't expect you to call me so early," she whispered and looked back toward the bedroom to see if Tyrone listened in on her conversation.

"I just got finished with Bible study and wasn't sure if you told me you had something else to do," he explained.

"Oh, I was coming to Bible study but Terri called me at the last minute and needed to talk about something. So, I decided to spend a little time with her."

"Is she alright?"

"Yeah. She's just a little stressed out from work and all."

"Okay, baby, but why are you whispering?" Randy asked.

"Uh… cuz we're at Barnes and Noble and I don't want to be too loud."

"Well, you and Terri enjoy yourself. I'll see you when you get home."

"Alright."

"Love you."

"Love you too, bye."

When Denise pressed the end button on her phone she thought Tyrone hadn't heard a thing until she looked up and saw him standing in the doorway of his bedroom with his arms crossed. *I know I just added fuel to an already blazing fire.*

Denise didn't say anything. She couldn't fix her mouth to, just got up from the couch and started putting her clothes back on.

"You just gonna leave. Just like that?"

"I gotta go," she replied and continued dressing.

"I see. Pastor Tate needs you." He laughed sarcastically.

"Don't even do me like that. You know I'm not in the mood. I got to go but do me a favor."

"What?" Tyrone asked.

"Grow up," Denise replied as she walked out of his condo and slammed the door as hard as she could. As she walked to her car, she figured she needed to slow down.

On her way home, Denise stopped over Terri's house so she could freshen up and get herself together before facing her husband.

Denise pulled into the garage next to Randy's car and, after she got out, quickly approached the door leading inside their house.

"Hey baby," said Randy. Denise jumped back a little.

"Oooh! You scared me."

"I'm sorry. I didn't mean to." He hugged Denise and removed her coat. Then, his eyes fell on her outfit. He looked at it, seemingly confused.

"What you got on, baby?" He twirled her around and caught a full glimpse of her.

Oh my God. I should've changed before I came home. He has never seen this. Okay...relax and take a deep breath. If I don't act guilty then he won't be suspicious.

"Something new I picked up. Do you like?" Denise turned around in a circle again to make sure he saw the two apple logos serving as her back pockets.

"That's hot, baby, but don't you think it's a little too revealing?"

"So you don't think it looks good on me?" she asked.

"No, I didn't say that, dear. The outfit looks phenomenal on you. It's just a little different than what I'm used to seeing you in. That's all."

You're used to seeing me in skirts that come all the way to the floor and jackets covering every inch of my upper half. But, to be honest, this is how I really want to dress. I don't even know why he trying to act like he doesn't like my get up. He knows he wants to rip this outfit off of me.

"Matter of fact, don't think I've seen you in something like it since we were dating," he replied as a smile crept across his face.

"I know. I wasn't really going to get it until I tried it on. When I saw it fit me really good, I decided to buy it."

"Oh. Okay," he replied nonchalantly. But she knew it bothered him.

"Babe, does it bother you, for real? Because, if it does, I'll take it back." *If he does have a problem, I will make it my business not to wear it around him again. But, I'm not returning it. I don't care what he says. I'll make him think I did, though.*

"Naw honey, it doesn't bother me. It's just different. Besides, if you looked bad in it, there would be a problem. But since you look great, keep it. I just can't promise to keep my hands off of you if you wear it out with me."

"You are so crazy," she continued and she kissed him on the lips before sliding past him to go upstairs and prepare for bed.

Chapter Six

"Randy, where are you going? I thought we're going to spend the day together before I leave with Terri for the weekend?" Denise asked as she saw Randy getting dressed so early in the morning.

"I'm so sorry, baby. But, I have a meeting at church that came up at the last minute. I apologize," he said as he slipped on a pair of socks.

"How long do you think it'll last?" Denise asked.

"About two hours or so," he replied. "But, I promise as soon as it's over. I'll be back." Randy walked over to Denise's side of the bed and sat down next to her.

"You know what, Mrs. Tate," he asked and Denise smiled.

"What," she responded as he grabbed her hand and kissed it.

"You are so beautiful, even when you first get up in the morning," he continued just as Denise took his chin and kissed him softly on his lips. "I am definitely the luckiest man in the world."

Denise was absolutely gorgeous. Her skin was a caramel complexion. She had hazel eyes and wore her hair short and naturally curly. She had dimples in her cheeks and a beautiful smile – the kind that would turn a homosexual man straight.

"No baby. I'm the lucky one. Babe, don't worry about rushing home. I think I'll go shopping today," Denise replied.

"Okay, honey. Have a good time and try not to do too much damage."

"I don't even know why you would say that. You know I always do." Denise smiled and kissed her husband again before he walked out.

Even though Randy often promised to be home as soon as his meeting ended, it never happened because there was always someone in need of prayer or counseling. So, before she knew it, it would be about six or seven when he made it back home. Denise didn't expect him to be back until later that evening. That's why she told him not to rush. She knew something always came up at the last minute.

Once Randy left, Denise thought about giving her sister Michelle a call. It had been a while since they talked to each other and even longer since she was at the church. So, Denise picked the house phone up off the cradle and dialed the number. After a few rings, the line went straight to voicemail.

"Hey sis, I'm just trying to catch up with you. Haven't talked to you and I'm worried so when you get this message call me back." She hung up and hadn't even sat her phone down when it rang.

"Where have you been? I've been trying to call you," Tyrone said through the receiver, sounding like he was in a hurry.

"Tyrone, are you forgetting it is only ten in the morning? I just got up not too long ago. What do you want?"

"To see you but you don't sound like you want to see me. What's up?" he asked while Denise rolled her eyes.

"I can't. I have other plans for today."

"What plans do you have that's more important than seeing me?"

She hated when Tyrone tried to act like he was so significant that she had to drop what she was doing to run to him. That's why she barely took his calls anymore.

"Believe it or not, I have a life and it sometimes fills up with things that don't involve you. So, when you can stop acting like a selfish little brat, call me. Otherwise, don't!" Denise hung up and finished getting ready.

She didn't have time to try to cater to Tyrone and the foolish games he always wanted to play. She figured he was furious about her hanging up on him but knew that, after he came to his senses, he would be back. It was as if he could never get enough. Denise tried her best to spend as much time as she could with him but even that proved to be insufficient.

Denise opened the door to her walk-in closet and picked out the new Dolce and Gabana jumpsuit she'd ordered from a catalog. She was happy to see it complemented her many curves and fit in all the right places. She decided to wear it to the mall since it was sophisticated enough to have on in public yet flashy enough that people would know she dropped some serious cash for it.

The doorbell rang while Denise applied her makeup. It startled her and she end up drawing a crooked lip line before jumping up and running down the double staircase only to see Mama Tate through the glass door. Thank God the window appeared distorted when looking through it because, the moment Denise saw her mother-in-law, her face twisted up. She was surprised Mama Tate came over knowing good and well her son was at the church. She knew where he was at all times. Even if she hadn't talked to him directly, she still knew. Denise often thought Alice was blessed with a sixth sense, some type of psychic ability allowing her to see right through a person and that scared her. That's why Denise made it her goal, when she was around her, to say as least as possible but somehow, someway she always manipulated and got herself right under her skin.

"Good morning, Denise. I'm surprised you're home this early. And on a Friday," Alice said as she walked right past her and took off her blue rain coat.

"I don't know why. I'm always home at this time of morning," Denise replied, noticing that Alice started with her sarcasm early.

"Come on, Denise. I call my son all the time, and most of which, you're not here. He says you're out running errands and doing things a wife should but I know different."

"What's that supposed to mean?"

"You're not taking care of my son and you know it! It's bad enough he has a demanding job then he can't depend on his own wife."

"Your son can depend on me. And I do take care of him!"

"Well, if you take care of him like you say then how come you're never home? You don't work. And by the looks of it, you're getting ready to go somewhere now," she continued while eyeing Denise from head to toe.

"Actually, I'm on my way to the spa."

"Denise, honey, don't get me wrong. I didn't come over here to be all in your business. All I'm saying is you have a good man and, if you don't do what you can as his wife to take care of him, you're just gonna make it easy for some other woman to move in and take your place."

Denise wondered how many times Alice would remind her that she had a good man. She knew just exactly what she possessed. She didn't need a constant reminder of how privileged she should be to be on Randy's arm. In fact, she doubted if Mama Tate thought about how lucky her son was to have a woman like her. She was one of the most beautiful, respected women in the city. So what if she had her cake and ate it too, she thought. What she did in her personal time was her business and she tried her best to be respectful to Randy's mother. But as she looked at Alice, she came closer and closer to saying some things she might regret later.

"Well, thank you for stopping by. I'll tell Randy you came over."

"That's okay, honey. I'll call him," Alice said as she left.

Denise's impromptu visit from her mother-in-law threatened to ruin her entire day. She was glad Alice left when she did because, if she stayed a second longer, there would've been major problems. By the time she pulled up to the mall, she felt ready to do some serious damage. She visited Cache', one of her favorite boutiques in the mall. It was the place where she brought all of her exclusive dresses and jeans. After picking up a couple of items from there, she moved onto Macy's. She brought the latest Gucci perfume before making her last stop at the MAC counter. The makeup artist pulled the newest colors out and Denise ended up buying all of the eye shadows she saw. In the process of turning to walk away from the counter, she bumped into someone.

"I'm sorry for not watching where I was going," she said without looking up.

"So, we meet again," a male voice replied. For a slight second, Denise stood there without saying a single word. At first, she thought she bumped into a complete stranger but the longer she stared, the more familiar he looked.

"I know you from somewhere, don't I?" she asked, trying to recall where they met.

"I'm Darnell. We met at the gym."

"Oh yeah. Now, I remember. I'm sorry. My memory can be so bad sometime," Denise said, recalling how she was attracted to him while thinking he seem to look even better in regular clothes.

"I guess your memory is a little bad because you were supposed to call me and never did," Darnell replied. "You didn't even come back to the gym."

"I apologize. So busy, I barely have time for myself."

"I understand. It happens to all of us," he responded then Denise sat her bags down on the ground and shook her hands.

"My bags are so heavy."

"I know you don't plan on carrying those around the mall do you?"

"Actually, I was just getting ready to take them to the car and try to figure out what I want to eat for lunch."

"Lunch does sound good right about now."

"Well, why don't you join me? That is, if you don't have anything else to do," said Denise.

"I would like that. Do you have a particular place in mind?"

"I know this nice, quiet place. It's up the street," she continued. Darnell carried Denise's bags to her car then he got in his and followed her to a place fifteen minutes up the road called Steamer's. Denise received three phone calls as she parked in a spot right in front of the building. She saw in the caller ID two calls from Randy and one from Tyrone. Rather than calling either back, she turned her phone off and tossed it back in the bag. She knew Randy probably called her to say he had something else to do or someone to visit and Tyrone basically called to get on her last nerve. She didn't have time to talk to either of them and whatever they wanted could wait until after her impromptu date.

Darnell opened the door and held her left hand.

"Thank you so much. That's nice of you," Denise replied as she held onto his hand and exited her car.

With a confused look on his face, he answered, "You're welcome."

Denise didn't know why he appeared that way, but at first, really didn't think anything of it until they were twenty-five minutes into their meal and he hadn't said too much. However, he kept glancing at her left hand until he spoke.

"Marie, can I ask you a question?"

"Sure. What do you wanna know?" Denise asked as she playfully pressed her lips together.

"Are you married?" Darnell stated while pointing to the massive rock she sported on her left hand's third finger.

"Am I married? No, I'm not married." Denise took a sip of her Sierra Mist.

"If you're not married then why do you have a ring like that on your finger?"

"Oh this." She held her had up and looked at it. "I've wore this for quite a while now. Seems like every time I go out, I run into some guy trying to talk to me and they are usually the ones who won't take no for an answer. But, when they glance down and see my ring, they run in the other direction," Denise lied. During times like those, she was glad she knew how to respond on the spot. The thought to slide it off while driving to Steamer's crossed her mind briefly but she forgot to actually do it.

"That's some kind of ring to wear only for appearance. It looks very real if you ask me," Darnell replied as he picked up her hand and examined it.

"Oh. It's real," Denise said as she smiled.

"You spent some serious cash on it."

"I must admit, I did drop some dough. It was a gift to myself, when I graduated from college."

"So, you're beautiful and smart." Darnell grabbed her hands and intertwined them with his. *I really can't believe he brought the lie I just told,* Denise thought. She did in fact go to college but never graduated.

"Answer me this question. Why aren't you taken," he continued but she shrugged her shoulders.

"I don't know. Guess I just haven't found the right man."

"The ones you've come across must've been completely stupid to pass a woman as fine as you up."

"You know, that's exactly what I tell myself." Denise knew she was being completely dishonest but couldn't help it. She felt like the less he knew about her real life, the better off. She hadn't run into too many men that were still interested in her upon learning of her marital status. So, she chose to keep that fact under wraps, especially since he seemed bothered by the ring.

"Honestly, I thought I wasn't going to see you again. But, I feel like bumping into you right now is... We were meant to see each other again."

"Maybe so. I really should've called you sooner."

"I'm not even worried about that. What's important is now."

They spent the remainder of the time eating and getting to know each other. By the time Darnell walked Denise to her car, she was almost certain she wanted to see him again.

"Marie, I had a really good time with you today."

"I enjoyed being with you too." Denise looked at her watch and told him she had to go.

"I hope this isn't the last time I see you," Darnell said.

"No, it won't be the last time. I'm going out of town for a few days. When I get back, we'll definitely hook up." Denise reached up and gave Darnell a hug and he pulled her in close to him. His muscular build mixed with the scent of his cologne turned Denise on, therefore she let go of his embrace before she did something impulsive.

"See you soon, Marie."

As Denise pulled her car in the garage, she saw Randy's truck parked next to hers so she reached in her glove compartment and took out a bottle of perfume she kept in case of emergency. She sprayed herself a few times to cover up any traces of Darnell's scent that may have rubbed off on her while they were at lunch. *Thank God for Armani Code*, she thought.

When she walked into the house, she found Randy sitting in the living room flipping through channels. She put her shopping bags near the bottom of the steps, kicked off her shoes, and then joined Randy on the couch and kissed him on his cheek.

"Where have you been?" he asked while continuing to flip through channels with the remote.

"Shopping. What's wrong with you? It seems like you're a little tense."

"Been calling you all day. You haven't answered once," Randy replied.

"I'm sorry but, when you called, I was trying on clothes. I couldn't answer it."

"You were trying on clothes for almost five hours?" Randy asked.

"No, I didn't try on clothes for that long. Come on, babe." Denise laughed it off but Randy didn't see anything funny.

"So, why didn't you call after you were done?"

"I wasn't aware that I had to."

"It would've been nice. My mother called this morning, told me she stopped by to check on you and you were on your way out the door."

Is he serious? He cannot be. Randy actually believes his mother came over here to check on me? He's got to be kidding. That old bird only came over here to be all up in my business. She wasn't the least bit concerned. Matter of fact she could care less.

"I left right after she stopped by. I told you before you left that I was going shopping so I don't see what the problem is."

"The problem is I was worried about you after I couldn't reach you. I was even more worried when you never called me back. It's a crazy world out here, Denise."

"Randy, I can't believe you're upset. I told you where I was going to be."

"It's not just that. I know you're leaving with Terri and I wanted to spend some time so I canceled some of the things."

"Now you're making me feel guilty because I wasn't here when you finally had time for me? I don't ever make you feel guilty for being away."

"What are you talking about, Denise? I'm not trying to make you feel guilty about anything."

"Well, that's what it sounds like to me. I'm just saying, I took today to do a little shopping before I leave. I would've never gone if I knew it would make you mad."

"Denise, I'm not mad. I'm not mad at all. All I'm saying is I would like for you to answer your phone while you're out, that's all," Randy said as he got up and walked out the room. Denise watched him as he exited and went up the steps.

What in the world is Randy's problem? She wondered.

Denise allowed Randy the head start to the bedroom and followed suite ten minutes later, giving him a couple of minutes to calm down. When she entered, he sat on his side of the bed with his face in between his hands. After seeing him in that position, she definitely knew something else going on with him.

"Baby, I'm sorry I snapped at you downstairs. I had a rough morning at church."

"Do you want to talk about it?"

"No, I really don't feel like it. I want to put everything aside and spend time with you before you leave tomorrow."

"I would like that," Denise replied as she walked over to Randy and pushed him back on the bed. Then, she kissed his lips. "I also apologize for not calling you today."

"Apology accepted."

Chapter Seven

"**G**ood morning sweetheart. I have something here for you," Randy announced as Denise sat up to breakfast in bed the following morning.

"Oh baby. You didn't have to go to any trouble and cook me anything."

"I didn't. Your favorite restaurant in the whole wide world did," he added. When Randy said that, she knew it could only be one place.

"Roller's?" Denise asked.

"Sure is," he replied and sat the tray table on her lap.

"Wow. What made you go there? I love Roller's."

"Me too babe. I don't know what made me get up and go but I'm glad I did. I miss their food."

Denise stared at her plate and reminisced about how much they used to go to *Roller's Restaurant* when they lived on the north side. They used to wake up every Saturday morning and get dressed early just so they could go over and eat. Mr. Roller served food like no other and he wouldn't stop until you were good and full. His Sunday dinners were in such high demand that Denise would sneak out of service just to place their order. If she didn't get a head start, his dinners were gone by the time church let out. Roller's had the best BBQ chicken, macaroni and cheese, collard greens, and candied yams money could buy, Denise thought as she picked up one of the two strawberries then fed them to Randy.

"Thank you so much. This is just what I needed," Denise said as she gave Randy a kiss. He put the empty tray to the side and wrapped his arms around her.

"What am I supposed to do all weekend without my baby?" he asked while planting small, sweet kisses over her face and neck.

"You keep on and I might have to cancel my plans."

"Now, that's a thought. I could cancel mine too. We can spend the whole weekend together," he replied and continued kissing. She pulled away from him slightly and smacked her lips.

"What was that for?" Randy asked.

"Now, baby, you know you canceling your appointments at the church is not going to happen. Besides, I'm only going to be gone for three days. I'll be back before you know it," she said. Randy wrapped his arms around Denise even tighter and planted a kiss on her forehead.

"I know but I'm gonna go crazy without you."

"You'll be okay."

"Okay well, I'm about to hop in the shower and get dressed before you and Terri leave. Why don't you join me?"

"Would love to but I'm still not finished packing and Terri's going to be on her way soon. You know how she is about being off schedule."

"Terri has never changed," Randy replied. "But it's okay, baby. Go ahead and shut me down. But just wait until you come back. I'm putting you on strike," Randy said as he crossed his arms like he had an attitude. Denise laughed.

"Randy, I highly doubt that. But, if you want to, try that when I come back. Give it your best shot," she continued while standing and walking pass him to the bathroom. Quite naturally, he followed.

While Randy showered, Denise packed up the rest of her things, called Terri, and then dialed her sister Michelle's number. However, she didn't answer so Denise grew weary. It was unlike her sister to not answer her phone or, at least, stop by with her two sons. It had been a while since she'd done either and Denise started to think something was going on that she didn't know about.

"Baby, can you do me a favor while I'm gone?" she asked Randy as he walked out of the bathroom wearing nothing but a towel wrapped around his waist and some baby oil on his upper body.

"Sure Denise. What is it?"

"Can you go over to Michelle's and check on them? I can't get in touch with her and I'm starting to worry."

"I'll stop over there after I leave the church today."

"And Randy…"

"What?"

"I just want you to know that you're not slick. Not at all."

"What are you talking about, sweetheart?" He looked at Denise as if he didn't know what she was referencing.

"You know what I'm talking about. Coming out of the bathroom with the baby oil all on your chest and only wearing a towel. I told you, you couldn't do it," she said just as her cell rang. Denise glanced at the number and pressed ignore.

"I can do it. You're the one who would have problem," Randy said as Terri beeped her horn outside.

"What's that supposed to mean?" Denise asked.

"Nothing. Have a good trip, babe."

When Denise opened up the front door, Terri stood on the porch tapping her watch.

"I'm so glad you are ready because you know how I am," she said.

"Girl if anybody do, it's me. That's exactly why I'm ready to go."

"Now, how long did you think we're going to be gone? It looks like you packed your entire closet," Terri stated while looking at the four bags of luggage.

"Whatever Terri, you know I can't help it. I over packed because you never know what we'll get into this weekend and I want to be ready for whatever." Denise handed Terri her big Louis Vuitton duffel bag and she put it in the trunk of her silver BMW 745.

Once they got in the car, Terri inserted the key in the ignition and drove around the circular driveway to leave while Denise's phone rang. She disregarded the call.

"Well, Denise, sit back and relax because this weekend we're going to have fun."

"You know I'm game," Denise replied, then put on her seatbelt. Her phone rang again but she glanced at the number and pressed ignore for the second time.

"Someone must really be trying to reach you because your phone has been ringing non-stop since you got in my car," Terri mentioned before Denise rolled her eyes and her phone rang again. Instead of passing it up, she answered it.

"Hello Tyrone," Denise said in a dry tone. She looked over at Terri who started laughing as soon as she heard his name.

"For a minute, I didn't think you were going to answer."

"I didn't seem to hear my phone," Denise lied.

"Well, to me it looked like you heard but ignored the calls," Tyrone answered.

"What did you just say?" Denise raised her eyebrows and asked.

"I said, you did hear your phone ringing but chose to not answer."

"Hold up, how is it looking like I'm dodging your phone calls. You can't see me."

"Yes I can. I'm right behind you," he replied then Denise quickly turned around and saw his car.

"What are you doing behind me?"

"I was out and about and thought I'd ride around for a while."

"So, what possessed you to just drive through my neighborhood of all places?"

"You live in this neighborhood?"

"Yeah!"

"I didn't know that, Denise. I was just passing through. Honestly," Tyrone replied.

"You mean to tell me you're driving around and just so happened to stumble upon me."

"That's exactly what happened."

"You must really think I'm stupid, Tyrone. I don't believe that," Denise said but he started to laugh.

"I guess I'm a bad liar. You caught me. I was driving around and thinking about you so I decided to see where you live. I never got a chance because I saw you in the passenger seat of your friend's car."

"You were that anxious to see where I'm living, huh?"

"I must admit. I was curious. And even though I didn't actually see your house, I must say I'm impressed with the community."

"I'm glad you're impressed but, if you don't mind, I have to go."

"Okay baby. Don't let me hold you. But, when you get a moment, call me. I miss you."

Denise didn't answer him back. She ended the call and threw the phone back inside her purse. Terri turned the music down and looked over at her friend.

"Girl, I don't see how you still talk to him. Tyrone would get on my last nerve if he was my man."

"You don't even know the half, Terri. He drives me absolutely crazy to say the least."

"Why do you still deal with him then?"

"I ask myself the same thing all the time. That is until I'm screaming his name. Then, I remember why I put up with him. And aside from all that, he can be really sweet sometimes."

"Okay, that was too much information."

"You asked."

"So that was him behind us in his car? I didn't know he knew where you lived."

"I had no idea. I never told him and he knows how I feel about that. We agreed he would never know."

"Well, I guess he didn't listen to that rule. Now, did he?"

"Tyrone doesn't listen to nothing."

"Sounds to me like Mr. Tyrone is lightweight crazy... if you ask me."

"No, he's harmless. Just a fool sometimes. That's all."

"Whatever you say, Denise," Terri continued while Denise's phone rang again and she answered it in a hurry. She couldn't believe Tyrone called her again. He began to annoy her beyond belief.

"Why do you keep calling me? I'll call you when I get a chance," Denise yelled.

"Hey, baby girl."

"Oh! Hey dad. I thought you were someone else," she said but rolled her eyes as she realized it was her father. She didn't want to talk to him either.

"It's so good to hear your voice. I haven't spoken to you in such a long time. How you been?" he said. Denise looked at the caller I.D. and saw her father called from a private number. *Oh, so now my dad has finally gotten smart. He knew there was no way I would've answered if his number popped up. I gotta start ignoring private calls too.*

"I've been fine, dad."

84

"How's my son-in-law?"

"He's good."

"How's the church been going lately?"

"Great. Our attendance is up three percent. I can't complain."

"That's just wonderful. Well, I was calling to tell you I love you and I miss you."

"Dad, you kinda caught me in the middle of something so..." Denise said as she tried to wrap up their conversation.

"Baby, I'm sorry. I won't hold you up. I'll just catch up with you another time."

"Okay."

"I love you, Denise."

"Goodbye dad," Denise replied and placed her phone in her lap. She crossed her arms and leaned her head back on the rest trying to relax from both calls since they sent her over the edge. She felt Terri looking at her so she opened her eyes.

"Why are you staring at me?" Denise asked.

"You already know. Why do you insist on talking to your father like that?"

"Because I have nothing to say to him. You know that."

"You cannot still be mad at the man for what he did in the past."

"Well, I am. I haven't had anything to say to him since everything between him and my mother went down. And for now, I would like to keep it that way." She gave Terri a look, indicating she was finished discussing her father.

"Denise, I'll get off my soap box. But before I do, just do me one favor."

"And what is that?" Denise wondered while Terri took her phone then turned off the power and tossed it on the back seat.

"This weekend, there will be no phone calls from anyone. All we're going to do is have fun the way we used to."

"I don't object to that at all."

The entire time Terri drove to Detroit, Denise tried to relax and rid her mind of the phone call she received from her father. But the harder she tried, the more the thoughts about him remained. Denise attempted to avoid her father's calls at all cost. There was nothing left for her to say to the man who was responsible for breaking their family apart. She remembered how good life was when her parents were married and he was the pastor of their church. They were one big, happy family. Her father was full of so much wisdom and good advice. So, in her eyes, he could do no wrong. He was always there when Denise or Michelle needed him and treated their mother like a queen. Denise had even decided to follow in his footsteps and attend seminary school.

As they traveled the highway, she thought back to the day Oral Robert's University sent her acceptance letter in the mail and she rushed over to the church to tell him the good news. She walked past the church secretary's office and looked in to see if she was there. And although her office door was open, it was empty. So, Denise walked past the office and made her way down the hall to her father's study. As she approached, she heard his voice intermingled with a woman's. She figured he was probably meeting with someone like he always did so she knocked on the door twice and opened it only to find her father with some woman spread out on the top of his desk. By the shocked look on his face, you would've thought he'd seen Jesus himself standing in the doorway. He was so pale that she thought he'd either pass out or use the bathroom on himself.

"How could you?" Denise asked as tears streamed down her face.

"Denise, I can explain."

For Denise, a partially naked woman was pretty much self explanatory. She didn't need him to tell her a thing because she was grown enough to know exactly what happened.

"I gotta get out of here." Denise said as he tried to approach her. She couldn't wrap her mind around the fact that the man she always loved and admired would do something sinful. She always considered him to be as close to perfection as one could get so for him to have an affair behind her mother's back hurt Denise deeply. From that moment on, she never looked at him the same. She didn't even look at men the same and vowed to never ever fully trust them again.

Chapter Eight

By the time Denise woke up, Terri was pulling into the parking lot of the Hilton. "Wake up, sleepy head, we're here," she announced as she parked under the car port.

"You mean to tell me I slept the entire way here?" Denise asked as she let out a yawn.

"Yes. You slept the entire four hours."

"I must've been more tired than I thought."

"Why you were tired? You were tired of those back to back phone calls."

Denise shook her head in agreement. "That's exactly why."

They were greeted by a tall, thin bell hop that looked like he could be related to Kobe Bryant. He smiled and winked while lifting their bags out of the trunk with ease and loading them onto his cart. Denise let him move away a little distance from them before she said something to Terri.

"Girl, he was winking at you hard."

"Denise, you know that boy don't even look like he's out of high school. But, I do think him winking was a sign."

"What sign?" Denise asked.

"It's a sign from God that we're about to have fun this weekend!"

Denise and Terri went directly to the desk where the clerk pulled up their reservation.

"Okay, here are both of the keys to the suite. Enjoy your stay." The woman smiled as she typed a few things into the computer and handed Terri a receipt. They turned and started walking in the direction of the elevator.

"Did I hear that woman correctly? She said we had a suite."

"Yes, you heard her right. I told you we were going to live it up and what better way to get started than with a fly room. We're staying in the penthouse... to be exact."

The elevator took them up to the eighteenth floor and once the doors slid open, Denise and Terri laid their eyes on their posh surroundings. The suite had everything you could ever want, complete with two bedrooms joined by a living room, a fully stocked bar, kitchen, and flat screen televisions mounted on the walls. The living room had a terrace that offered breathtaking views of the city and both of their bathrooms had Jacuzzi garden tubs. From the minute that Denise saw their room, she knew their weekend would be off the hook.

"So what do we have planned?" Denise asked.

"Go and get dressed, we about to hit the club," Terri responded. Denise gathered her bags and took them into her bedroom. She opened up her duffel and placed all of her outfits on the bed so she could decide on something to wear. After about ten minutes of looking through her clothes, she chose her all black bebe jumpsuit with some black Jimmy Choos.

Terri saw Denise emerge from her bedroom looking fresh to death and began to scream with excitement.

"Okay mama! You looking like you ready to party." Terri checked out her outfit.

"You looking good too. I think that's why we're best friends." Denise smiled as she watched Terri strut back and forth like she walked the catwalk on America's Next Top Model.

"Girl, we look good to be thirty-five." Terri slapped hands with Denise.

"Get it right. I'm almost thirty-five. I'm not there just yet. But while we're on the subject of my birthday, I really pray Randy does something special for me and doesn't forget like he did last year."

"The way you two got into it, I don't believe he'll ever forget your birthday and I'll make sure he does something special," Terri replied while they both stood in front of the full length mirror.

"You gotta admit, though. We look good to be our age."

"Oh, most definitely. I know some women would give anything to look the way we do." Denise slapped hands with Terri and they left for the club. She had to admit, they did look exceptionally well to be in their middle thirties. When they went out, they were always mistaken for being in their twenties. With absolutely no waist, Denise stood about five feet four inches tall and was thick in all of the right places. Terri was built similar to her petite friend but was a whole lot taller which made her appear thinner. She was an inch away from being six feet and could easily be a model.

Terri drove Denise to Club Lavish, one of the most popular clubs in the Detroit. And when they pulled up in front for valet parking, there was a line wrapped around the side of the building onto the next street.

"How did you hear about this spot?" Denise asked as she saw big groups of people walking toward the entrance.

"Remember my friend Chanel? She's a bartender up here now," she responded. Denise stepped out of the car and Terri handed her keys to the valet attendant.

"Do you see how many people are out here? I bet it'll take us at least two hours to get in." Denise clutched her purse under her arm as a guy with a bright Coogi outfit brushed past her and almost knocked her off her feet.

"No it won't. I have the hook up. Watch this." Terri walked up to the bouncer who was posted at the door with his arms folded. He was so tall and all muscle, as if he could crush you by just looking at you.

"Can I help you?"

"Yes, we are personal guests of Chanel."

"Oh yeah, she told me you would be coming. Go in and she'll meet you at the bar with VIP passes." He pulled back the rope and allowed Denise and Terri to walk into the club past the whole crowd of angry people who were mad because they didn't have connections.

"That's what's up." Denise smiled as they entered.

"I told you I got this."

They walked through the crowded dance floor to the bar where Terri spotted her friend from back in the day pouring a round of shots for a group of young girls who looked like they just became drinking age.

"Chanel," Terri called. She looked up and recognized her friend.

"Hey girl, what's up?" She reached over the bar.

"Nothin much. We just came up in here, tryin' to get the VIP hookup."

"What's up girl? I haven't seen you in a long time." Terri's friend reached over too and they hugged.

"It's so good to see you." She reached under the bar and handed Terri two passes attached to lanyards and they put them around their necks.

"Girl, it's hype up in here," Terri said as her eyes scanned the club.

"It's always like this but it's even more live in VIP. So, go have fun. I'll send ya'll some drinks up there."

"Cool," Terri said.

As they walked up to exclusive area, The DJ put on *"Get Me Bodied"* and the club went crazy. Everyone who was sitting made it out to the dance floor, including

Denise and Terri. When they arrived in VIP, it wasn't any different. They danced and mouthed the words as Beyonce sang her upbeat record. Denise loved to dance and often missed going out to the clubs because Randy sure wasn't going to take her. He wouldn't allow the first lady to be caught in one of those clubs and Denise knew that, as his wife, it wasn't the proper thing to get caught up into anyway.

As the song played, she became lost in her own little world as she seductively moved her hips to the beat. She closed her eyes and just enjoyed DJ's selected play list. She was so caught up in dancing and having a good time that she didn't even notice a guy came up behind her and started moving with her. When she turned around, she noticed the tall, light skinned man with the dreads dancing to her rhythm.

"Excuse me, I'm sorry. I just started dancing with you without even asking, but I just couldn't resist."

"No, it's cool. I don't have a problem with you dancing with me but, if you would've touched me, we would've had a problem," she stated over the music and he laughed at her boldness.

"I like you already. My name is J.D." He stuck out his hand.

"Marie," she responded.

"Nice to meet you." As the song went off, J.D. followed Denise off the dance floor and slid beside her in the booth where they previously sat. Denise caught a glimpse of the diamond encrusted watch he wore and she knew he had money. She could feel he was a powerful man just as she could feel him rubbed on her legs. She hoped that by the end of the night, she would get a chance to see what he was really worth.

While on the dance floor, Denise didn't get a chance to really see him. But once he sat directly under the light, she got a full glimpse of just how good he looked. He had skin the color of honey with dreads falling to the middle of his back and secured into a ponytail. His smile was captivating and his blue eyes made Denise want to stare into them the entire time they talked. He kind of reminded her of Shemar Moore.

"So, tell me. What's a sexy woman like you doing in a place like this?"

"My best friend and I are in town and we wanted to check it out. Why? Do I look out of place?"

"No, you just carry yourself different. You know, with class. Very different from the regular crowd of women."

"You must come here all the time."

"You can say that. I'm part owner." He smiled proudly.

"For real? I didn't know owners came out and partied with everyone."

"A lot don't, but I do. Think it's a good way to bring publicity to the spot."

"That's cool." Denise checked out his ice game and admitted she was impressed. Both of his ears held diamond studs and he wore a platinum chain with a diamond-encrusted cross while his wrist was frozen with a diamond bracelet. Just from his jewelry game alone, she knew he definitely racked in a nice cash flow. They talked for the rest of the night and when the DJ announced the last song, Denise knew she had to make her move or she wasn't going to have a chance at all.

"What I need to do for you to leave this club with me tonight?"

Denise was surprised at his boldness. She was usually the aggressive one. She loved being in control but liked how he flipped it.

"What makes you think I want to leave with you?"

"We've talked the entire night."

"That don't mean anything."

"Look me in my eyes and tell me you don't want to."

Denise looked into his eyes and attempted to say no but, as hard as she tried, she couldn't open her mouth to say it - the same way she fell for Jackson years ago.

"Let's go. I have my Range Rover parked out front."

Denise bit her bottom lip, stood up, and followed him out the club.

The next day, Denise woke up with an excruciating headache. She knew the throbbing sensation was the result of the hangover. She hadn't anticipated it being that bad. She rolled over and buried her face in the pillow, hoping it would stop but that only made matters worse. Then, she could hear Terri walking around the sitting area of their penthouse suite while every noise Denise heard made her want to vomit.

I swear I'm never drinking shots of Patron again. I guess it has a way of really sneaking up on you. After she left the club with J.D., they ended up going to an after-hours spot. Then once that closed, she ended up going to his high-rise apartment. In that small amount of time, she consumed two Long Island's and three more shots of Patron.

Terri opened up Denise's bedroom door and let a whole burst of light into the room. Denise swung her arm over her eyes.

"Come on and get up. You've been sleeping too long. We're supposed to be on vacation," Terri said as she came and plopped down on Denise's bed.

"Please don't do that. I feel like I'm going to gag."

"What you drink that's got you tore up?" Terri asked.

"Shots of Patron and Long Island."

"No wonder you're so messed up."

"I swear as long as I live I'm never drinking like that again."

"So did you have fun with J.D.?"

"Of course," Denise said before explaining the night's events while managing to sit up. "We talked and drank..."

"Would be safe to assume there wasn't much talking once you got to his place," Terri inquired. Denise smiled halfway and then put both of her hands on her forehead.

"I can't believe you had sex with him."

"Why can't you believe it? We're here on a weekend getaway. You said it yourself. We're having fun. That's all I'm doing, having a little fun. There isn't any harm in that. Now, is there?"

"You consider your one night stand just having a little fun?"

"It's just fun while we're here. I know this is going to sound silly being we're not in Vegas and all. But, as far as I'm concerned, what happens in Detroit stays in Detroit."

"If you say so, Denise. Well, it's time for me to have some fun too."

"What do you have in mind?"

"Let's go shopping."

"I'm down, as soon as I sober up a little." Denise stood up and, while watching Terri shake her head, walked toward the bathroom then closed the door.

Chapter Nine

Denise returned from the weekend in Detroit and found a note her husband left on the kitchen counter. It read: *Denise, when you get this, please come to the church. We need to talk. It's very important. Randy.* She folded the crumpled paper up and stuffed it inside her purse. Her mind began to race with thoughts as she hurried to the garage, got in her car, and drove toward Oakdale Baptist. She wondered what Randy wanted to talk about and why he felt a need to have her rush over. On the way, she racked her brain trying to it figure out but wasn't able to come up with anything.

Her Rolex read 1:10 p.m. as she pulled into her first lady parking spot. She walked through the side entrance where the executive offices were located and ran right into the church secretary who carried a pitcher.

"Good afternoon, Mrs. Tate. How are you?" she said.

"I'm blessed. Where are you rushing off to?" Denise scrunched her eyebrows together with a confused look on her face.

"Oh, they're having noon day prayer in the main sanctuary and I was taking them this water."

"Is my husband in his office?"

"He's back there typing up his sermon notes."

"Okay," Denise replied then walked in the opposite direction. The door to his office was already open. She entered and found Randy at his computer, working as if his life depended on it. She tiptoed until she stood right behind his chair, bent down, wrapped her arms around him, and kissed his cheek. "Hey, baby. I see you're busy."

Randy got up from his chair and hugged her. "You know me, I'm just trying to stay on top of things. I'm glad you're home." He leaned down and greeted his wife with a kiss. "Did you and Terri enjoy yourselves?"

"We had a really good time. You miss me?"

"Come on, now. Don't even have to ask. You know I did."

"So, what do you want to talk about?" she questioned. Randy sighed, then grabbed Denise by the hand and led her to the couch where they sat down.

"I did go over to your sister's like you asked but she never came to the door."

"Was she home?"

"Her car was outside so I know she had to be there."

"Did you try to call her?"

"I called both numbers and it just kept sending me straight to voicemail so I tried to track Jimmy down."

"He never called you back either?"

"No. Not at all."

"I'm about to drive over there." Denise attempted to stand up and walk away but Randy held her arm.

"Wait. There's more."

"What?"

"Yesterday, I went to BW3's for some wings and it was extra crowded because the Browns were playing the Steelers. But, guess who I ran into?"

"Who?" Denise asked.

"Jimmy. And he wasn't alone either."

"He was with another woman?"

"I'm sad to say he was."

"Did he see you at all?"

"He saw me and tried his best to explain himself but it was already too late. That woman was all over him," he continued while Denise opened up her purse, took her keys out, and stood up. "Where are you going?"

"To see about my sister," she said before she stormed out of the church.

Denise jumped in her Lexus and headed toward Michelle's house. She was glad her sister only lived fifteen minutes from the church so it wouldn't take her long to get there. And as soon as she parked in front of the townhouse, her phone rang so she looked at the screen. When she saw the area code alone, she knew it was Darnell.

"Hello," Denise answered with an attitude.

"Hey beautiful. I was calling to see how you were doing."

"I'm fine, but I really can't talk right now."

"Why? Is everything okay?" he asked.

"I'm dealing with a situation with my sister, but other than that, I'm alright."

"I was calling to see if you wanted to get together tonight for dinner, but I understand if you can't."

"That sounds good, but I'll have to call you later on just to confirm everything."   "You know my number, so when you decide, just give me a call," he continued then was silent but spoke again. "And, Marie, I really hope to see you. I have a surprise."

"What kind of surprise?" Denise responded.

"You'll just have to see me to find out," he said then ended the call.

Continuing about her business, Denise got out of the car and walked up the short, grassy path to the front door. The lawn looked like it hadn't been cut in two months. If someone was just passing by her sister's house, they would've probably thought no one lived there. She rang the doorbell and waited but there was no response.

"Michelle!" she shouted. "I know you're in there. Open up." Denise knocked as hard as she could.

"Michelle! I'm not going anywhere until you answer this door."

Denise stopped pounding and could hear footsteps then saw the curtains move, confirming her sister was home. She knew Michelle tried to make it appear as if she wasn't there, but Denise planned on staying until she decided to let her inside. Finally, after five minutes, Michelle opened up the door in her bathrobe and hair rollers.

"How did you know I was here?" she asked.

"I know you better than you know yourself. Besides, your car is parked right there." Denise pointed and walked in the door and looked around the room. "What's going on? This house is a mess."

"Nothing. I'm fine. It's a little junky because of the boys. You know how they are sometimes," Michelle replied and started picking up the scattered clothes and toys.

"Why are you lying to me? You don't look like everything is fine. You've got to be the biggest neat freak I know. What's really going on?" Denise interrogated.

"Trust me. I am fine." Michelle rolled her eyes and sat on the couch. Denise wondered why she wasn't opening up to her when they usually talked about everything.

"Come on, Michelle. Is something going on I need to know about?"

"No. I told you everything is fine."

"Something is obviously wrong. It's written all over your face."

"No. It's not."

"Well, where are my nephews at?"

"They're at Jimmy's mom. Why?"

"That's how I know something is definitely wrong with you because you always send them away when something ain't right."

"That's not true, Denise. They just wanted to spend some time with their grandmother. That's all," Michelle replied and looked away.

Something was definitely wrong with her baby sister and she was determined to find out what happened. Michelle was the type of person to keep quiet about everything, even when she was going through something. She wouldn't tell Denise when she had a problem until things were usually out of control. She always tried to act like nothing was wrong but Denise knew her like the back of her hand. She knew the reason she shut herself up in the house like that was all due to her husband.

"Where's Jimmy?" Denise sat down beside her and Michelle put her head down.

"He left again. You know how he is." She began to cry.

"What happened this time?"

"He started back drinking a couple of months ago. But even still, things were good between us, or so I thought." Michelle grabbed tissue from the Kleenex box sitting on the coffee table and wiped her eyes.

"What happened?"

"A week ago, he came home from work and we got into an argument about money I asked for to pay some bills. Then, right in the middle of the conversation, he said things weren't working out between us and left."

"When was the last time you saw or heard from him?"

"When he left. But, look at this." Michelle handed her a little card.

"What is it?"

"A card from some woman talking about she had a good time and loves him."

"That's crazy, sis," Denise uttered. Ever since she married him, he's been nothing but trouble, she thought. His wandering eye, frequent visits to the bar, and "disappearing acts" always proved to be overwhelming for Michelle.

When they first got together, she was in college pursuing her dream of becoming a journalist and Jimmy was finishing up his bachelor's degree in business until Michelle became pregnant with their oldest son, Junior, and their plans were put on hold. Back then, Jimmy had a good head on his shoulders and Michelle's best interest at heart. He desired to make them a family and wasn't satisfied until he had her at the altar saying "I do." Somewhere along the way, it seemed like he forgot what that actually meant.

Michelle tried her best to be patient with him and stay by his side, hoping to really make their marriage work, but she grew tired of the roller coaster ride. They had been married for almost seven years and Jimmy managed to be unfaithful to her since year one. Time after time, he cheated on Michelle until she determined it was enough then somehow he always found a way to get back into her heart.

She always held onto the hope that the next time he would really change his ways and wouldn't dare do anything else to add to the list of things he had already done. However, the more she took him back, the more he would mess up. It would be as trouble followed Jimmy like a magnet.

Michelle opened up her mouth to continue their conversation but became choked up with emotion and couldn't speak. So, Denise went to the kitchen and got her sister a glass of water and an Advil.

"Take this." Denise dropped the tiny pill into her sister's hand then watched her drink the entire glass of water.

"I mean, how can another woman say she loves my husband? It just breaks my heart to know that he probably said it back to her." She started to cry again.

Denise shook her head. She hated to see her baby sister going through so much pain, all at the hands of her no good husband. He had left Michelle and the kids so many times, Denise wondered what it was really going to take for her sister to get enough strength to leave Jimmy. She was tired of her everything he had done to her and prayed that, this time, Michelle would heed the signal and move on with her life.

"So what are you going to do, Michelle?" Denise asked.

"Honestly, I don't know. In the past, I've always believed I wouldn't tolerate Jimmy cheating and disrespecting me. But now, that I'm in this situation again. It's easier said than done."

"I understand but you know he is totally out of line."

"I know, sis, but it's a hard situation when you love someone. And, we do have two kids together."

"So, you're basically telling me you're trying to stay with him even after he did all this to you and the boys?"

"I really don't want to have to get a divorce and put my sons through that kind of trauma. You remember how ugly mama and daddy's divorce was and we were older. I feel my kids deserve a stable environment."

"And that's one in which their father is an alcoholic, cheats on their mother, and their mother is so depressed she can't even take care of them. Yeah, Michelle, that's real stable." Denise's sarcasm made Michelle's nostrils flare.

"That was very harsh."

"I'm just being honest. What you think is stable is really not all that secure and you feel you're doing your kids a favor. What you could be doing is hurting them."

"And how am I hurting them?"

"You're hurting them by trying to remain somewhere that's clearly not healthy. You may believe they don't know what's going between you two but your kids are smarter than you think. They know and it's affecting them more than you know," Denise replied.

Michelle sat there with her face in her hands. "So what am I supposed to do?"

"It's time to start living for you. If you make the choices and include you in the equation, everything else will fall into place. I understand you are trying to make decisions with the boys in mind but you need to also do what's going to make you happy. You don't need to be with someone who's running around drinking and cheating. Your boys deserve more than a mother who's too depressed to take care of them."

When Denise finished her miniature speech, Michelle wiped tears from her eyes.

"You're exactly right. I guess I never looked at everything like that."

"I'm going to stay and help you clean up. Then, we can go and grab a bite to eat."

"That's okay, Denise. I know you're busy. I'll get it. Then, I'm going to go and get my sons."

"Are you sure?"

"I'm fine. I'll pull everything together," Michelle replied and gave her sister a hug.

"Call me, if you need anything." Denise picked up her keys off the coffee table and walked to the door.

"I will and thanks, Denise. If it wasn't for you, I would still be lying around feeling miserable," Michelle commented before saying goodbye.

Denise left feeling good that she got to the bottom of things and glad she'd convinced Michelle to get herself together. She hated to see her sister go through affair after affair and continue to stay with Jimmy. She felt like her sister deserved someone better and hoped Jimmy's temporary exit from her life would become permanent so the right man could come along and sweep her off her feet. She knew if her sister actually divorced Jimmy, her nephews would be upset but eventually they would get over and move on with their lives. Besides, she didn't want them to grow up and look at their dad as an example because he was not necessarily a good role model for them. More than anything, she prayed Michelle would see it as a way out of such a turbulent situation.

Denise arrived home and didn't see Randy's car in the driveway or in the garage then remembered that he said he would be home by the time she came from Michelle's. However, the house was completely empty. She picked up her Blackberry and call Randy's via the speed dial feature.

"Hey. Where are you at?" Denise asked.

"Oh! Hey baby. I'm out with the deacon. He came and picked me up from Oakdale. We're meeting with one of the contractors that are going to be adding onto the church. Are you at home?"

"I just walked in. I left Michelle's not too long ago."

"How is she doing?" Randy asked.

"Better."

"That's good to hear."

"So are you coming home any time soon?"

"Well, I'm going to be out for a while. Still waiting for the guy we're meeting with to arrive. Do you want me to bring you something home to eat?"

"Naw honey. I think I'll go to Terri's and see if she wants to go and get something."

"Well, I'll call you when I'm on my way home."

They ended the conversation but, instead of Denise putting the phone down, she called Terri.

"Hey girl. What's up with you?"

"Nothing. At home. Trying to catch up on some of my cases. What you doing?"

"I called to see if you want to go out to dinner with me since Randy is busy."

"I wish I could but I am completely swamped. I'm going to have to pass this time."

"Okay, well call me when you get a chance."

Denise ended the call with Terri and the phone started to ring as soon as she put it down.

"Hey Marie. Did I catch you at a bad time?" Darnell asked. She smiled when she heard his voice on the other end.

"No, you didn't. I was actually just getting ready to call you."

"So are we on for tonight?"

"I think so. My schedule actually just opened up."

"Perfect! Does dinner around seven sound good?"

"Yes, that sounds fine."

"I'll pick you up around six thirty."

"No. That's okay. I'll just meet you."

"I'll just see you at The Blue Wolf Tavern then."

"You will."

Denise went upstairs and into her walk-in closet where she began looking through her clothes. She wanted to find the perfect outfit to wear out to dinner with him. After an hour of searching for an outfit, Denise picked a pair of Seven Jeans and purple button down shirt. She wanted to keep her look simple yet sexy and the pants she picked along with the matching shoes did the trick. Denise took a shower, got dressed, put some mousse in her already curly hair, and applied her makeup.

By the time she was done, she looked nothing less than a million bucks. When she checked her phone, she had three text messages. One was from Darnell and two were from Tyrone. Darnell's text let Denise know there had been a slight change of plans and he told her to meet him at an address he provided. The two messages Tyrone sent were about hooking up later that night. She sent a text message to Tyrone telling him they would have to see each other another time because she was busy. Then, she responded to Darnell and informed him she was on her way.

Chapter Ten

"I'm glad you didn't mind about our slight change in plans," Darnell said as he opened up the door to his duplex apartment.

"No. It's okay, Darnell," Denise replied in the most courteous manner she could muster up. But she couldn't believe he had the nerve to invite her over to his place when he clearly lived in a neighborhood that looked dangerous.

This man has got to be insane having me come over here and this neighborhood looks the way it does. Doesn't he know I drive a brand new Mercedes? I know he don't think I drive a ninety-thousand dollar car and live in the hood like him. There were people hanging out on the corner when I turned onto his street. And once I stepped out of my car, a couple of dudes who had the nerve to whistle at me. I didn't even bother to turn around. I just grabbed my Valentino bag, hit the lock button on my key chain twice, and prayed this man would answer his door promptly.

Darnell led her up the steps and into his immaculate apartment where he motioned for them to sit down on his couch. Denise sat down slowly and clutched her purse. She had to admit, at first glance, Darnell's apartment looked the complete opposite of the neighborhood and she was slightly impressed.

"Are you okay, Marie? You look a little uncomfortable."

"I'm fine. Why would you think that?" she asked as she tried to laugh it off.

"Well, you don't look like it. I mean, you are fine but you know what I mean," he rattled. Denise reached out and stroked his hand.

"I'm good for real. I must admit, I was a little nervous pulling on your street but you do have a wonderful place here," she replied.

"Thank you. I appreciate it. Making my apartment look extra nice was the least I could do to make up for my cousin playing me," Darnell said as he smiled exposing dimples Denise had never seen before.

"Your cousin played you?"

"To say the least. I moved out here from Detroit. Since he lives here, I told him to find me a great place for a good deal. Somehow, he assumed I wanted to reside in the hood."

"Wow, so you're cousin is responsible for this apartment?"

"Exactly. He's the one to thank. I'm actually planning to live here until my lease is up. Then, I think I'm going to find me a nice place out in the Austintown area."

"It's beautiful out there. You'll find you a place." Denise said just as she heard an oven timer ringing.

"Our dinner must be ready."

Darnell and Denise got up from the couch and he took hold of her hand then led her into the dining room that was connected to the kitchen. The table was set up for a quiet, romantic evening for two. A bright white table linen was draped over it while a vase full of white roses sat in the center. To top the entire decoration off, Darnell accented the table with gold and white candles that gave off a sweet aroma. Even the dinner napkins were folded precisely and wrapped with a gold ribbon.

"This looks wonderful. Must've taken you a long time to complete."

"Actually, it only took about fifteen minutes."

"It looks great."

Darnell pulled out her chair and proceeded to the kitchen. He brought in a pan of lasagna straight from the oven then cut two pieces before he sat down to join her.

Denise bowed her head and said a prayer of thanks for her food then looked at Darnell who had his arms folded across his chest.

"Aren't you going to eat, Darnell?"

"Yes, but I want you to taste it first and let me know what you think."

"Oh. Okay." Denise picked up her fork and knife and cut into the lasagna. She put the piece in her mouth and instantly a smile crept across her face.

"This is really good. Where did you learn to cook?" she asked while chewing.

"My father. He's is a chef back home."

"Not only can you decorate, you can cook too? So, what's the catch?"

"There is no catch. My father is a chef and my mother is a professional decorator so I picked everything up while helping them with their catering service."

"So why didn't you stay up there and continue on with the family business?"

"I tried. Even went to culinary school for a while but that's not my passion."

"What is it?"

"I really love working as a personal trainer."

"I see." Denise reached across the table and touched Darnell's bulging bicep.

"It's the type of job I would work even if I wasn't getting paid."

"Really?"

"Yes, I would. I enjoy seeing the dramatic changes a person's body goes through once they get serious about their health." Darnell poured some wine and took a sip, then continued. "So, since you've asked me a couple of questions, I feel it's only fair if you allow me to ask you one."

"Go ahead, whatever you wanna know." Denise smiled and drank her wine.

"Why isn't a beautiful and intelligent woman like yourself not taken?"

Denise slightly choked. She put her glass down and cleared her throat.

"You don't beat around the bush do you?"

"No. Actually, I was never raised like that. Just a direct kind of guy."

"Honestly, I'm a firm believer in the Bible saying that says 'he who finds a wife, finds a good thing' so I guess you can say he hasn't found me yet," Denise replied and quickly glanced down to check her finger, making sure she left her wedding ring and band at home. She let out a sigh of relief when she realized she took it off.

"I don't want to sound corny, but I do think I've found what I've been looking for," Darnell said as he leaned over the table and kissed her.

"Is that right?"

She pulled her lips away just enough so that she could move her mouth. Denise couldn't even fix them to say anything else because Darnell moved in and started to kiss her again. Then, the attraction she'd already felt for him seem to intensify. She knew, at the rate they were going, they would end up in his bed and Denise wasn't opposed to the idea. But the doorbell rang and interrupted them.

"Who is that?" Denise asked as she became annoyed with whoever insisted on ruining such a great moment.

"Oh, remember how I told you I had a surprise for you earlier?"

"Yes," she replied as Darnell left her where she stood and walked to the door.

"This is my surprise. Marie, I want you to meet my cousin. Tee, this is Marie."

Denise was speechless as she saw Tyrone standing before her with his nostrils flaring. He stood still, looking at her like he wanted to attack. If looks could kill, Denise would've been gone.

Darnell noticed the nonverbal communication Denise and Tyrone gave each other and raised his eyebrow.

"What's wrong, man? You look like you're mad."

"What did you say her name was?"

"Marie. Why?"

"Her name isn't Marie. It's Denise."

"Wait a minute. Denise... Your Denise?" he uttered. Tyrone shook his head and it made Darnell turn and look at Denise.

I don't know why this dude is looking at me like I'm a child in the principal's office. The way he's staring at me makes me feel like I'm about to be scolded by my parents or something, Denise thought.

"I can't believe this. So everything was a lie?" Darnell asked.

"What do you mean everything?"

"Our dinner at Steamer's. Our date tonight. It was all a lie?"

"No, it wasn't. I really enjoyed spending time with you. It wasn't."

"You lied about your name. Lord knows what else."

"I bet she left out the part about her being married too," Tyrone added. Denise rolled her eyes at him and wished he would shut his mouth. He already spoiled their entire evening and was making it worse by continuing to talk.

"You're married?" Darnell shouted then waited to see what she was going to say. Before she could even respond, Tyrone moved closer to them and answered for her.

"Yes, she's married. Don't you see the permanent tan line on her ring finger? It's pretty hard to cover up." He held her hand up to give Darnell a better look but she yanked it away.

"I'm leaving," Denise grabbed her purse and walked out the door.

She wasn't about to sit around after everything that just happened. Never in a million years did she think Tyrone and Darnell were related. There were some definite similarities she saw in both of them but probably would've never picked up on them if they weren't in the same room together. Denise slid her key in the ignition and started up her car. But, before she could pull off, Tyrone opened the passenger side door and was half-way inside.

"Get out! I'm leaving!"

"No! Not before I talk to you," he harshly spoke. Denise put her car in reverse and turned to look at Tyrone who didn't seem phased by her announcement.

"Tyrone, I am about to back out and would appreciate it if you get out my car and shut the door. And if you don't move, I don't have no problem with running you over." Denise tried to push him out but he didn't move an inch.

"I'm not leaving until I talk to you."

"Is that how I can get rid of you? Fine. Go ahead," Denise replied. Tyrone shut the car door as hard and as loud as he could, which caused Denise to become annoyed. "Are you done having your little tantrum? I thought you wanted to talk."

"So, how long has this been going on between you and my cousin?" he asked as he looked straight ahead while cracking his knuckles.

"That's none of your business. And for your information, I didn't even know ya'll were related."

"What you mean none of my business? Whatever you're involved in and the fact this is my cousin makes it my business."

"Whatever Tyrone. You're so possessive for no reason. I've just had dinner a few times with Darnell and you're acting like I'm screwing him."

"I don't know that."

"Since you're so nosey, I haven't had sex with your cousin at all."

"You may think I'm possessive but I don't have to possess what I already own."

"What's that supposed to mean?" Denise asked as she crossed her arms over her chest.

"Denise, whether you believe it or not, you belong to me. Always have and always will."

"You're trying to tell me you own me like I'm some piece of property?"

"I didn't stutter. I said you belong to me."

Denise started to laugh as she heard Tyrone proclaim his ownership over her. She hadn't heard something so ridiculous in all her life.

"Well honey, I'm sorry but I have news for you. I'm already married so you, nor your cousin, own anything. My husband owns all this. I don't know what you're talking about. You must be crazy or something," Denise replied. She could feel her heart beginning to race as she finished her sentence.

"Oh, I'm crazy? I'm crazy? I'll show you crazy," he ranted.

Then, in one swift motion, Tyrone lifted up his hand and slapped her with the back of it. The look in his eyes suggested he was beyond pissed. And when Denise looked over at him, she didn't even recognize the man sitting seated beside her.

"Get out! Right now!" She reached and pushed him out of the car.

"Denise, wait a minute. I'm sorry. I really didn't mean to do that. I was just mad." Tyrone tried to explain but Denise didn't even care. She shut her car door and put the car into reverse so fast she could've got whiplash. As she sped off, she was in shock over Tyrone putting his hands on her. The right side of her face stung as she drove and her eyes couldn't stop watering from the force of the blow. Denise flipped down the visor and checked herself in the mirror. She didn't have any marks yet, but she knew it was only a matter of time before one appeared because her face was already turning red.

She picked up her phone and tried to call Terri but she didn't answer. The only other person she could think of was Jackson however his line went to voicemail so she just placed her phone back in her bag and cleared her mind for the rest of the ride home. Her face was red and swollen by the time she arrived. There was no way Denise could play it off because it was too late. *Randy is going to really think something is going on. I have to come up with something before I walk in the house,* she thought.

Denise took her time out in the garage before she entered the house. She even managed to find a small bottle of liquid foundation she kept in her purse then turned it upside down and dabbed a tiny amount onto her face. She attempted to blend it over her cheek but the more she rubbed it in, the crazier her bruise looked. Denise took a deep breath and walked in the house.

"Hey baby. It's good to see you home at a decent hour. I honestly thought that you would still be out with the deacon," Denise said as she walked in and saw Randy reading *The Vindicator* at the kitchen table.

She bent down and kissed him quickly.

"Actually, our meeting wrapped up pretty early," Randy replied, then stopped Denise to look at the emerging red mark on her face.

"What happened to you, babe?"

"My purse strap was stuck in between the seat and when I pulled on it, it flew up and hit me right in my face." Denise even demonstrated how the strap supposedly struck.

"That's a pretty nasty mark, honey. Looks like you've been in a fight with someone." Randy laughed and Denise chuckled along with him, thinking if he only knew that he had hit the button right on the nose. "Well, if I was you, I wouldn't carry that purse again because it seems to have some issues with you."

Denise grin, thanking God she got away with that one because it was close.

The next day Denise called Terri at her office and told her she needed to talk to her so Terri agreed to clear her schedule. When Denise arrived, she was completely covered up in a sweat suit, hat, and a pair of Christian Dior shades.

"What's up with your little get up today?"

"Girl, you don't even want to know."

"What you talking about? I've never seen you look like this. And why do you have those shades on inside the building?" Terri inquired. Denise took a deep breath and removed her sunglasses. When she turned, Terri's mouth dropped to the floor.

"Oh my God! What happened?" Terri came from around her desk and touched the side of Denise's face.

"You'll never guess."

"What? Tell me." Terri asked and Denise did. "I can't believe he would do something like that to you. Hold up. Yes I can. Tyrone's a lunatic," she continued.

"Tell me about it."

"So, what did Randy have to say about your new beauty mark?"

"Nothing," she said, then explained what she told Randy and how he believed her.

"You gots to be kidding."

"Why wouldn't he? I am his wife you know."

"You and your little lies. Just when I think you can't come up with another one, you never cease to amaze me.

Here. Look, what I found." Terri reached on her desk and picked up a black photo album then handed it to Denise. She blew a coat of dust that clung to the top of the album off. "It's from back in the day."

Denise started to flip through it. She smiled as she came across photos of when she had long hair and some of Terri when she was hired at the law firm. Denise laughed when she came across a picture of Terri and other associates from her office.

"Go head, I already know why you're laughing," Terri responded.

"Look at you with these long braids, looking like you were in *Poetic Justice*." Denise turned and showed it to her.

"I don't care what you say. Those Janet Jackson braids were in style."

"Well, if they're the style, why don't you have them now?"

"You know they went out in the nineties. Besides, you know my job ain't even havin' it." Terri flipped through and turned the page around to show Denise.

"Look at who's in this picture with us."

"Jackson," Denise said as she studied the photograph.

"I bet that took you down memory lane."

"It sure does. It was taken the first night we met each other."

"Have you talked to him lately?"

"The last time we talked was right after he came in town about two months ago."
Denise pulled out her phone and began pressing numbers.

"Who are you calling?" Terri asked as she watched Denise.

"Him." Denise momentarily put their conversation on pause waiting for Jackson to pick up his phone but he never did. "He must be working today." Denise hung up.

"Dang, you know the man's work schedule by heart?"

"It's not like that. He usually answers when I call so he must be really busy."

"I'm pretty sure he'll call you back."

"If he doesn't call back by tomorrow, I'm going to Akron and surprise him."

"You go up and see him unannounced like that?" Terri asked.

"I've done it a couple of times before. I think it's about time to see him again."

"So, you're birthday is three days away. Are you excited?"

"I guess you can say that but I think I'll be even more once I buy me something to wear."

"Where are you going to go?"

"I really don't know. But since I plan on going up to Akron, I'll shop up there."

"Now, the next question I have to ask is, since you're going to see Jackson, are you going to have any time to shop?"

"The way Jackson and I are when we're together, I might just have to wear something out of my walk in closet," Denise joked before she decided to go and cook dinner, hoping to spend an evening with her husband.

Chapter Eleven

Denise awoke to the sun peeking through the sheer drapes covering her master bedroom windows. The brightness of the sun's rays caused her eyes to open up wide, leaving her no choice but to get up and embrace the day. She felt like it was definitely going to be a good one as far as she was concerned. She was two days from her thirty-fifth birthday and had decided to make the necessary trip up to Akron so that she could find something to wear. This was also a perfectly good excuse to pay Jackson a visit.

She tried to call him again right after she left Terri's office then two more times before she went to bed yet he still didn't pick up his phone. She became more eager than ever to see what he'd been up to since he hadn't returned any of her phone calls.

"I wish I could go up to Akron with you today but I have to still work on my sermon for Sunday morning," said Randy.

"I know, babe, but that just means you have to take me up there the next time." Denise wrapped her arms around Randy.

"You have a deal, Mrs. Tate." He kissed her lips.

When Denise first announced "the Akron shopping trip" to Randy, he tried his hardest to go with her. At first, he told her his schedule was free and clear so she was disappointed because it appeared as though her plans would be canceled. But apparently, he looked at the wrong calendar as the one in his office at their home didn't always correlate with the one at the church. Once Randy told Denise that he wasn't able to go, she knew her plans were still in effect. Before she left, she seductively whispered everything she planned on doing to Randy when she returned into his ear.

"Now, you have me messed up for the whole entire day."

"That's what I wanted to do." She smiled.

"This day better go by fast."

"Don't worry. I'll be back before you know it."

Denise gave her husband a kiss and left the house. She put her purse on the front seat of her truck and slowly pulled out the driveway. With all of her bases covered at home, she pulled onto I-76 and headed toward Akron. The sun was shining so bright that she flipped the visor down to shield her eyes from the light. She pushed the eject button on her disk player then removed Yolanda Adams and replaced it with Ne-Yo's, *Because of You,"* CD that she had just brought from Wal-Mart.

As she cruised in her Lexus on the highway, the smooth and breathtaking vocals blasted through the speakers. Denise could hardly wait to get up there and see Jackson. Her body had become overwhelmed with anticipation as she pulled into the housing development where he owned a beautiful, three-bedroom, contemporary style home complete with an outdoor fire pit and an in ground swimming pool.

Denise pulled up in Jackson's driveway and saw his Bentley GT Coupe parked in its usual spot, which meant he probably just arrived from work. She smiled as she parked right next to him. She missed him like crazy and couldn't wait to see him because, of the men Denise had been with, Jackson seemed to be the most understanding. He never demanded too much of her time while he took their relationship for what it was and nothing more. His easy going personality and laid back spirit is what made Denise continue to see him.

As Denise walked up his cobblestone walkway, she noticed an array of flowers that were planted, covering the entire length of the walkway.

"Since when Jackson plant flowers? He's afraid he might mess up his Armani suit," she said to herself as she walked up to the door.

She could see Jackson through his living room window sitting on the couch watching ESPN. She knocked several times before he answered.

"You are the last person I expected to see. What are you doing here?" he asked.

"Why, I'm not welcome anymore?"

"No I didn't say that. Come in," Jackson said while peeking outside as if he was checking for something before he shut the door behind Denise.

"What's wrong with you and why are you acting nervous?"

"I just thought I heard something."

It was apparent something made Jackson extremely nervous. Just by looking at him, she could tell something bothered him. Small beads of sweat ran down his forehead as they sat in the living room. Then, he kept getting up from his seat, walking over to the curtains, and looking out the window. Denise sat there for a minute studying his actions and couldn't quite put her finger on it but knew something was different.

"No, I'm fine. So what brings you over my way?"

"I missed you. That's all. Realized it's been a while since I've seen you. Then, you haven't been returning any of my phone calls. So, I decided to surprise you." Denise tried to wrap her arms around Jackson's neck and kiss him but he pulled away.

"Yeah, it's been a little while." He glanced over at his watch and made his way back over to the window, then looked out of it again.

"What's wrong with you? Why are you acting all weird? I thought you would be happy to see me."

"I am. I just didn't expect to see you today. Right now."

"What's going on?" Denise questioned but wasn't able to receive an answer because the doorbell rang.

Jackson left Denise in the living room and hurried over to answer it. When he opened the door, a tall, thin, light-skinned woman who carried a little girl on her hip walked in. The child immediately jumped out of her arms and ran to Jackson.

"Daddy, Daddy, I missed you all day!" the little mocha colored girl with long ponytails shouted as she wrapped her hands around his leg and he picked her up.

"I missed you too, baby girl. Give me a kiss," he replied and she did as told.

"Honey, your daughter's been talking non-stop since we left the daycare. Saying you're taking her to ride her bike in the park," the woman spoke as she walked up to Jackson and kissed him as if she didn't see Denise. After Jackson stole a couple of quick pecks before letting her go, she finally looked past him into the living room where Denise stood.

"Oh, hello," she said, seeming unsure of what to say as she looked at Denise.

"Hi, my name's Denise." She stepped forward and shook the woman's hand.

"Baby, this is Denise. One of my good friends."

"Oh okay." She smiled as if she was relieved.

"We haven't seen each other in a while so she wanted to stop by and say hello while she was in town."

"I don't think I remember hearing about you, but Jackson had a lot of close friends in college. It's so nice to finally meet you."

"Denise, this is my wife."

When Jackson revealed that, Denise felt like she'd been hit with a ton of bricks.

"It's been that long. I didn't even know you were married, Jackson."

"We've been married for three years now," Jackson's wife responded as she showed the massive wedding ring.

"Yes we have," Jackson replied and smiled at Denise.

"You know what? I think I'm about to leave. I didn't mean to intrude." Denise made her way to the door trying to escape as quickly as possible.

"Wait! It's okay. I was just about to cook dinner so you're more than welcome to stay. Ain't that right baby?"

Jackson let out a nervous chuckle and then continued to lie.

"I know she probably wants to but you gotta get going, right?" Jackson looked at Denise as if he begged her with his eyes to leave. Just to be devious, she stood in the door way to think about it quick second but decided not to for the sake of the little girl who stood in between them.

"Yes, I have to get going. Got some shopping to do," Denise somberly said.

"It was nice meeting you. You're welcome in our home anytime. Have a safe trip back."

Denise walked out and the woman shut the door. Denise chuckled to herself as she got in the car and left.

Here this woman was being all friendly and welcoming me like I was a first time visitor but, little did she know, her man already welcomed me into every part of their house, literally. Jackson even made me feel right at home in their bed. And, the nerve of him to sit there and lie to his wife right in her face. Everything within me wanted to expose him right then and there in front of his family but it wasn't worth it. Thank God I have a couple new outfits to pick from in my closet because this has definitely ruined my little shopping trip.

Over the next two days, Denise didn't know too many details about what they were doing to celebrate another year of life. He told her to just sit back and enjoy the festivities, whatever that meant. So, the morning of her birthday, she woke up to breakfast in bed then a day of special treatment at *In and Out Beauty Salon,* which Denise was not opposed to at all. This birthday was already proving to be way better than her last and she had a feeling it was only going to get better as the hours went on.

After she got her hair done, a manicure, and pedicure, she returned home to get dressed. When she arrived and went into their bedroom, Randy had a gift sitting on the bed waiting for her. She opened the box to find a diamond necklace, a pair of earrings, and a bottle of her favorite perfume, Gucci.

Randy is going all out this year. I wonder what he has planned next. I really hope he takes me to a nice restaurant.

It didn't take long for Denise to take a bubble bath and get ready. Before Randy could even blink twice, she walked down the steps in a little black dress that he had never seen before.

"You look absolutely stunning," Randy said as he met her and helped her down the last three stairs.

"Do you like this dress? It's something new," she lied.

"It looks great on you."

"Since I don't know where we're going, I didn't know what outfit to put on," Denise replied as he helped her put her coat on.

"You still haven't figured out where I'm taking you?"

"No. Can't you see I'm trying to throw you some hints?"

"Baby, don't worry. I have something special planned for you tonight and I believe it will definitely make up for last year."

During the entire drive to their destination, Denise kept quiet and tried to come up with an exact place but, every time she thought of one, all Randy did was laughed and told her she wasn't right.

"Honey, you're never going to figure it out. So, just sit back and relax," Randy said as it seemed as if he would pull onto the highway. However, he didn't.

"Where are we going?" she asked as she noticed him driving in the direction of the church.

"I forgot I have to stop by the church and grab something real quick."

"Okay. But, aren't we going to be late for dinner?"

"No. We're right on time."

As Randy pulled into the parking lot of the church, Denise noticed several cars.

"Why are all these cars here? Isn't choir rehearsal over already?"

"It was supposed to be a half an hour ago unless practice is running late," Randy answered then parked in his spot and turned the car off.

"How long are you going to be?" Denise asked.

"I shouldn't be long. But, why don't you come in with me."

"Okay babe."

Randy opened the door for her and helped her out. When they walked into the church, Denise expected the choir to be belting out one of their songs but; instead, she didn't hear anything. It was so quiet that the tapping of her stilettos on the marble floor resounded loudly.

"I know we saw those cars in the parking lot so why is it dead in here?"

"I don't know. Let's go see where everyone's at." Randy opened the door to the fellowship hall. It was pitch black.

"It's obvious no one's in here," she uttered.

Randy ignored Denise and led her into the dark room. The minute she stepped in, the lights came on then everyone jumped up and shouted, "Surprise!"

Denise looked around the room and saw various church members and even her best friend, Terri.

"So, Denise, I wanted to do something very special for you that I had never done. What better way to celebrate than to have a party with our church family. So, what do you think?" he asked as he took her coat off and handed it to a woman from the church who hung it up.

"It's nice, Randy. Thank you." Denise hugged him and rolled her eyes behind his back. She knew Randy went the extra mile and tried to do something extra special, but she never imagined he would throw her a party at the church. It was the last place she had planned to be on her birthday.

"I'm glad this was a surprise for you. If you excuse me one moment, I have to go to the kitchen and check on something."

Soon as Randy left, Denise scanned the room in search of her best friend. She spotted Terri across the room talking to one of the choir members, who just so happened to be a client of hers.

"Can I talk to you in private for a second?" Denise asked.

"Sure," Terri answered and followed her into Randy's office then shut the door. "First, before you say anything, Denise, I did not know Randy was planning something like this for your birthday. I know this is not your usual style."

"I must admit this is definitely not something I would've wanted to do on my birthday. But, that's beside the point. I brought you in here to tell you the latest news."

"What's happened now?"

Before Denise said anything else, she opened the door to make sure no one was coming down the hallway and then she closed it back.

"Remember I told you I was going to Akron to visit Jackson?"

"Yeah, so what happened?" Terri asked then Denise explained.

"What? Get out of here."

"No, if I'm lying, I'm flying. It completely shocked me to find all this out," Denise said, then went on to discuss what happened after his wife came home.

"Maybe, it's God's way of telling you to just stick with Randy because crazy things happen when you mess around with these other men," Terri rationalized.

"I don't think God is telling me that." Denise shook her head and laughed.

"Have you talked to Mr. Crazy Man since your little altercation?"

"No, but he's been blowing my phone up as usual."

"Are you planning on talking to him?"

"Not really. But, who knows. You never know with Tyrone and me. Let's get back to my little party before Randy starts looking for us."

Denise and Terri returned right as Randy walked out of the kitchen with some of the food. They were getting ready to sit down at one of the tables when Sister Daphne, one of the nosiest women in the church, approached Denise.

"Happy Birthday, first lady," she said and extended her arms out to hug Denise.

"Thank you, sister," Denise replied and tried to walk past her but she held onto her arm. She knew Sister Daphne only did that when she had gossip on somebody or was about to say something crazy so she figured it was one of the two.

"I also want to say your dress is very pretty, however, I don't think it's quite fitting for a pastor's wife to be parading around showing her flesh to the parishioners. It's not the right image, if you know what I'm saying," she replied in a low voice so no one could hear her.

Denise stared at the old woman who smiled at her like she was her best friend but she knew this woman was far from it. From the moment Randy was installed as pastor, Sister Daphne served as a constant nuisance to Denise. She had been responsible for stirring up mess and drama at the church and Denise couldn't help but feel that she secretly wanted her husband behind her back. She always made smart comments toward Denise but, when it came to Randy, she treated him like gold.

"I understand exactly what you're saying, but I am at liberty to wear whatever I want. And if my husband doesn't have a problem with it, then neither should you." Denise rolled her eyes and walked away, leaving the sister standing there with her mouth open. That put a smile on Denise's face.

Randy signaled to Denise to join him at the head table so he could bless the food. Afterwards, he pulled out a chair and they sat down at their own private table.

"Why aren't we going up to get our food, baby? I'm hungry," Denise asked as she pointed to the church member who was already in line.

"Don't worry, honey. This is your special night and the kitchen staff will be serving us personally," he explained. Denise smiled and sat back in her chair. "I meant to tell you my mother called and said they can't make it tonight. My dad is not feeling well so she decided to keep him home. She apologizes."

I'm not surprised. I don't know why he thought she was coming in the first place.

"It's okay, Randy, I understand." Denise kissed her husband on his lips and caught Daphne staring at her while she did it. To add more insult to injury, she leaned in and stole another kiss. Daphne rolled her eyes and turned her attention away from them.

"Wow, I'm getting two kisses and you haven't even seen your gift yet."

"What did you get me?"

"You'll see soon enough," he responded while one of the women from the kitchen brought out three covered up porcelain plates and set two of them in front of Denise and one in front of Randy.

"Why do I have two plates?"

"I don't know. Why don't you see," he replied and winked at her. Denise opened the first one and found it filled with all of her favorite foods such as Filet Mignon, asparagus spears, and a baked potato. Her eyes looked toward the plate that she hadn't yet uncovered. She pushed the one to the side and slid the other in front of her then removed the cover off. Immediately, she saw a teal box with a silk white ribbon. She opened it to find a pair of beautiful diamond earrings.

"Randy, these are so pretty. They're from Tiffany's."

"Anything for you, Denise. I'm glad you like them."

Denise removed the earrings she wore and put the new ones in her ears.

After her birthday dinner, Randy and Denise walked to the car.

"Denise, I have to run in my office for a second before we leave. I'll be right back."

She nodded her head and Randy shut the passenger side door then walked back in the church. While Denise sat there waiting, she thought about how her special evening. She actually ended up enjoying herself.

The phone vibrating in her black python clutch startled her. She picked the phone out of her clutch and saw Tyrone's number flashing across the screen.

"I don't know why you're calling. I don't want to talk to you," Denise said to her Blackberry before putting it back in her purse. It sounded again as she closed up her purse and, when she looked at Tyrone's number, she quickly pressed ignore then set it in her lap. No sooner than she overlooked it, Tyrone called again. Denise figured the only way he would stop is if she talked to him.

"Why are you calling me? Knowing you're the last person I want to..."

"I know you're still mad but I need to talk you."

"About what? Tyrone? As far as I'm concerned, there's nothing you can say..."

"We have a lot of things to discuss. I want to make things right between us."

"Well go head. Talk. I haven't hung up yet," Denise replied and rolled her eyes.

"Not over the phone. I would rather see you in person,"

"Whatever you need to say to me can be said now. Besides, the last time I saw you, you gave me a mark I'm still covering up." Denise looked up and saw Randy coming out of the church.

"Look, Tyrone, I gotta go."

"Denise, I promise if you come over and see me tonight, it'll be cool."

"Alright. Alright. I'll come over in a little while. I gotta go, bye." Denise erased her call with Tyrone as Randy got in.

"Who were you talking to just now?" Randy asked as he started up the car and drove off.

"Michelle just called. She wants me to stop over tonight."

"Do you want me to drive you over there?" Randy asked.

"No, I mean it's okay. You can go home and once I change my clothes, I'll just go over there."

When Denise and Randy arrived at their house, she decided to change into a pair of sweat pants with the matching shirt and got into her car and drove to Tyrone's. She knew she probably shouldn't have went after what happened the last time they were together but knew he would not leave her alone if she didn't at least make an attempt to see him.

Chapter Twelve

Denise pulled into Tyrone's driveway and turned her cell phone off before she walked up to the front entrance. She only knocked one time before he opened.

"You waiting by the door for me," Denise said as she stepped pass him.

"I was actually passing by when you knocked. I'm glad you could make it, though. Where you tell your husband went?"

"None of your business! I came over because you said you needed to talk. So, if you have nothing to say, I can leave," Denise replied coldly.

"Don't. I want to talk. I want to apologize for what happened between us at my cousin's house. I was out of line, had no business putting my hands on you."

"Is that what you call an apology?"

"I am sorry, Denise. I would never put my hands on you like that again. I really do apologize," he continued. She stood face to face with him and looked in his eyes. She could tell by his expression he was sorry, but wasn't sure if she wanted to absolve so soon. She crossed her arms and remained still without saying anything. If he wanted her forgiveness, he would have to work for it.

"I know you're mad. I understand if all you want to do is walk out and never speak to me again. But, I wanted to tell you I love you." Tyrone moved toward Denise and tried to pull her closer to him but she pulled away. All the anger and coldness she harbored turned into tears as she jerked back from Tyrone's grip.

"I'm sorry and I will never do that again." He wiped the water from her cheeks then placed his lips on hers while grabbing her behind. She attempted to resist but couldn't bring herself to do it. What made her mad turned her on at the same time. She couldn't understand, for the life of her, why she kept coming back to him when he took every opportunity to push the limits. Before she could even gather her thoughts, Tyrone led her to his bedroom and she kicked off her peep-toe heels.

"I don't know what comes over me sometimes. I've been going crazy without you," Tyrone said as the climbed in bed. He held her in his arms.

"I admit. I missed you too. But that can't ever happen again. And just to let you know, I've only had dinner with him. That's it," Denise said then gave Tyrone a look suggesting she meant business.

"It won't. I just got a little carried away. I know what went on. We talked. It's cool."

"Tyrone, that can't... You want my husband to find out?" Denise asked.

"Maybe not that way. But, he's going to find out sooner or later." Tyrone smiled.

"What's that supposed to mean? You're gone run and tell him?" Denise lifted up, stared at him then proceeded to put her shoes back on.

"I mean, I want to be with you. This sneaking around. Not knowing when I'm going to see you again. It's making me go crazy. But, don't worry. I'm not trying to get us caught. You don't have to worry about that," he said while pulling her back unto the bed. Then, the sexually arousing things Tyrone did with his tongue convinced Denise to relax and she remained with him for a few more hours. She honestly didn't know how he would react before going there but was glad it turned out positive.

When Denise left, she booted up her phone to find seven voice messages from her husband. She wondered what he wanted and why he called so many times before going into her voicemail and listening to the first one.

"Baby! When you get this! Please! Call me back! It's an emergency!" Randy's voice echoed and Denise's heart raced as she continued to listen. "Denise! Where are you? Dad had a massive heart attack! They rushed him to St. Elizabeth's! Call me!"

Denise almost swerved off the side of the road as she operated the phone while driving but regained control and turned the car around. On her way to the hospital, she prayed for good news because she wouldn't be able to live with herself if something happened to her father-in-law while she was fooling around with Tyrone. When she arrived at the hospital, she tried to call Randy as she parked but he didn't pick up so she left a message.

"Hey honey. I'm at the hospital. Call me back," she said, figuring he saw her number but needed time to step out into the lobby. She waited in the car for ten minutes and still hadn't heard from him, so she walked into the lobby and up to the front desk then asked the receptionist about Randy Tate Sr.

"Second floor. Cardiac Intensive Care Unit," the older woman responded. Denise turned walked toward the elevators. As her shoes hit the linoleum floor, her heart raced. She pressed the button and leaned against the wall. She closed her eyes and took a couple of deep breaths, hoping that would calm her nerves. As she inhaled and exhaled, she silently prayed for him to be all right.

The elevator doors opened and her eyes spotted the Cardiac ICU sign so she walked over to the door and tried to open. Because it was locked, she rang the doorbell then a short, light skinned nurse with her hair pinned in a bun answered. Denise explained who she wanted to see and asked if he was in that unit.

"May I ask who you are to him?"

"I'm his daughter-in-law, Denise Tate."

"Yes, he's in our unit. But, I'm sorry. Visiting hours is over for the evening."

"I can't even go and see him? I'm immediate family."

"Under normal circumstances, you could. But, right now, he needs all the rest he can get."

"Is he going to be okay?" Denise's eyes welled up.

"He got here in just enough time. But the heart attack he suffered is very serious so the next twenty-four hours is going to be critical. We need him stable."

Denise could no longer hold on to the tears she tried to suppress while the nurse rubbed her and gave her a tissue from her scrub pocket. However, it seemed like the more Denise wiped, the more she cried. Normally, she wouldn't be caught dead like that in front of someone a stranger but it she couldn't help it.

"I understand how you feel. My father had a heart attack a year ago."

"Is my family still here?" Denise tried to look through the window and see if she saw a familiar face hanging around in the hallway.

"Yes. His wife is still here. But last time I checked, she was dozing off to sleep."

"That's okay. Don't disturb her. I'll go home and be with my husband."

"We will call you with an update as soon as the doctor makes his rounds," the nurse explained as Denise moved toward the elevator which was already opening.

During the drive home, Denise attempted to call Randy again but he still didn't answer. She even dialed the house phone and it just rang too. With that, Denise assumed he either decided to visit with his brother or was passed out from exhaustion. Then, when she opened the garage door and saw Randy's Cadillac parked in its usual space, she figured he was asleep.

As soon as she stepped foot in the kitchen and dropped her purse and keys on the counter, Denise slid off her shoes. The house was completely dark and silent. It was so quiet she could hear her own heartbeat as she walked through it. Since nothing was on downstairs, she continued to think he was probably in the bed counting sheep so she tiptoed and crept up the steps. The last thing she wanted to do was wake him up. With each step she took, she tried to be even quieter since he was such a light sleeper and the slightest noise woke him. And just as Denise was almost up the stairs, several lights suddenly turned on.

Denise looked over her shoulders in the direction of the living room and saw Randy sitting in his recliner, fully dressed, with his arms crossed.

"Why didn't you return my message, Denise?"

"Baby, I am so sorry. As soon as I got it, I came over to the hospital."

"I called you over four hours ago!"

"I'm sorry... honey but I just got your first message a little while ago."

"That's because your phone was off."

"It accidentally turned off when I was at my sister's. I didn't notice until I was walking out the door."

"Why didn't you call me back? I'm sitting in the hospital not knowing if my father gone live or die. I'm worried half to death and don't know where my wife is at?"

"Baby, I am so sorry. I know you were worried sick."

"So, where were you?"

"I told you. Over Michelle's. With her and the boys."

"And, you accidentally turned your phone off?"

"Yes, I apologize. I really didn't know it was off," she continued. Then, with her hands, Denise cupped both sides of Randy's face and leaned in to kiss him but, before their lips connected, he pulled away, stood still, and shook his head.

"That don't sound right. Something isn't adding up, Denise," Randy said while staring into her eyes.

"What do you mean?" Denise played dumb.

"You said you were at your sister's with your phone turned off. You never turn your phone off. Where were you, Denise?" Randy crossed his arms and remained in the position. Denise unzipped her leather jacket and placed it on the couch.

"I told you already. What's with all the questions?"

"I dunno. Were you really with your sister?"

"Okay, Randy. What are you trying to get at?"

"I wonder if you were really over Michelle's. Or somewhere else."

"Come on! Are you serious? What, you think I'm cheating on you or something? Is that what you think?"

"You tell me. I didn't say it. So are you?" Randy asked then watched her closely.

Denise looked at him in disbelief. She couldn't believe he actual had the nerve to call her on the carpet about being unfaithful, even though it was as true as the word of God. His allegations actually caused her to laugh sarcastically as she answered him.

"I can't believe you would actually accuse me of cheating on you. You know I would never... I love you. But to be honest, this don't even sound like you."

"What's that supposed to mean?" Randy raised his eyebrows.

"This all Alice's doing. She's is the one who put that in your mind? She thinks I've been messing around on you since day one."

"This has nothing to do with my mother. I would prefer you left her out of it."

138

"Why not? You know she was the one always speaking bad things about me. Her main goal is to break us up. Always has been and always will."

"No, don't try to shift the focus to her because we wouldn't be having this discussion had you answered my calls. I just can't understand how your phone accidentally turns off and you neglect to check it for four hours. And I just wanna know the truth about where you were. That's all"

"Randy, I told you the truth, baby. I wouldn't turn my phone off on purpose. I was with my nephews. And my sister," Denise said soothingly as she walked over to try and hug him from behind. Again, he pulled away from her.

"I hear you but then again, I don't. This is not the first time you've been missing or haven't answered your phone. It was okay the other times. But, for some reason, I feel like there is something you're not telling me." Randy walked away from where she stood and up the steps when Denise ran and tried to block him from going any further.

"Randy! I'm telling the truth! Why are you…"

"You were unreachable for hours and I'm supposed to believe you're with Michelle."

"That's where I said I as at."

"And that's your final answer?" Randy asked as if he was a TV show host.

"Yes," she stated then attempted to open her mouth again but he interrupted her.

"You know what? I've had a long night. I'm going to bed. " Randy left Denise standing in the middle of the staircase with her bottom lip hanging to the floor. She realized he was furious and didn't know what might happen next so she left it alone.

The next morning, Denise awoke to Randy giving her the silent treatment. He didn't even make an effort to greet her, which was odd for him since it had been his daily ritual since they'd married. Denise ignored the silence between them and carried on with making him a huge breakfast. She could tell that he was still mad but hoped the meal would smooth things over. Once the feast was ready, she set the table and called upstairs for him to come eat. He didn't answer but she knew he would be shooting down as soon as his nose caught a whiff the aroma floating through the house. Like clockwork, Randy appeared fully dressed and sat across from her at the table. He picked up his plate and served himself as if she wasn't present. Denise allowed him to fill it up before she spoke, unbelieving the silence lasted as long.

"Come on, Randy. You haven't said anything all morning. You're still mad?" Denise asked as she searched for an indicator in his demeanor.

"Are you ready to tell me where you were last night?" He stopped chewing his food and sat his fork down then gave Denise his undivided attention.

"I told you, at Michelle's. My phone turned off by accident. I rushed to the hospital as soon as I could!" Denise's tone of voice rose slightly as she answered him.

"So you're still sticking to the same story, huh?" he asked then chuckled. Denise was caught off guard by his sudden outburst. Already nervous and clueless to where the conversation was headed, she felt her mouth becoming little dry then picked up her glass of orange juice and took a generous sip.

"It's not a story, babe. That's where I was."

"Well, why when I called her no one answered. I called Terri too and she hadn't seen or heard from you." Randy crossed his arms while a lump grew in the middle of Denise's throat, making it hard for her to open up her mouth. She literally felt like she was up against a wall with no way out unless she thought of something quick.

"I don't know, Randy. Where is this coming from?" Denise finished her statement unsure of what to say or do next. Their entire argument she had been unable to come up with anything good enough for him to believe so she resorted to the next best thing, her acting skills. As she stared into her husband's eyes, tears began to roll down her face like Niagara Falls as she sat there in silence. She knew Randy didn't like to see her crying and, if he saw it, then maybe the situation might turn in her favor. As she carried on her little charade, he didn't say a word until she wiped her tears with a napkin.

"Why are you crying, Denise?"

"I'm hurt. I love you so much and your father, I wish I could've been there. The one time I miss your calls this happens. And I don't know why we didn't hear Michelle's phone. I'm sorry, baby. I love you. I would never go outside my marriage and it makes me sick to even think that's what you may believe I'm doing." Denise pretended to hyperventilate and get even more upset as she emphasized every word and syllable. Randy observed how Denise was on the verge of passing out and let out a loud sigh as he cleared his throat.

"Okay, calm down. I see how upset you are. Look. I don't know what's goin' on but I don't like to see us in this state. So, let's forget about this right now. I'm going up to the hospital to sit with my mother for a little while."

Denise watched as Randy got up and walked over to her. He lightly kissed her forehead, grabbed his keys, and left through the garage.

Chapter Thirteen

Denise rolled over in their king size bed and Randy was not there. His side of the mattress was ice cold. She got up, put on her robe, and went downstairs to see him sitting in the living room packing his clothes as he prepared to leave for a minister's convention. He didn't even notice her enter the room.

"Hey baby. Why didn't you wake me? I would've fixed you breakfast." Denise walked over and hugged him from behind but he acted as if he never heard a word. Instead, he continued to fold his underwear.

"I didn't want to. My ride is on his way so I'll grab something at the airport."

"Are you sure? I can put something together for you real quick." Denise wrapped her arms around him and leaned in close to give him a kiss. He gave her a quick peck and then picked up an entire stack of shirts and placed them in his suitcase.

"I'm fine," Randy replied as a horn beeped outside. He took a big sigh. "That's my ride. I have to go. I'll give you a call when I touch down in Atlanta. I love you," he continued. He picked up his bags and walked over to the door. Denise followed him so he kissed her again and left.

Denise smiled as she opened up the curtain and waved goodbye to Randy and his associate pastor. She knew her husband was still somewhat upset about her "disappearing act" three weeks before even though they agreed to move on. She did and said anything in order to get back in Randy's good graces, including spending more time with his mother. So, with him out of the door, she grew ecstatic at the thought of being footloose and fancy free for seven days. She had some tension she needed to relieve and, for a week, she wouldn't have to tell her husband where she was at or doing. Denise anticipated the convention ever since the night of their argument because it was a big one with some of the nation's leading pastors and evangelists, so she knew he would be too consumed to worry about it once he arrived. As she turned around and walked back into the dining room, her house phone rang.

"Praise the Lord. You've reached the Tate's residence," she answered.

"Denise, I'm glad I caught you. I thought you would be out shopping," Terri said.

"No. Not with everything that's been going on lately."

"What is it?" Terri continued.

"Do you have some free time? This is definitely a spa moment."

"All afternoon. Why?"

"Meet me at Casal's at one."

"I'm there," Terri said. They ended the call then Denise got dressed for the day. She put on a light gray Juicy Couture jogging suit with her black Chanel shades then was out the door in a flash.

As she drove through her community, she could smell one of her neighbors chopping up fresh wood for a fireplace, while midst was in the air as it surely left its trace on all the trees lining the streets. The leaves were beginning to turn all different shades and colors and fall off. Denise rolled down her window halfway to feel the breeze and was glad she decided to dress warm. The spa wasn't a long drive away so she pulled into its parking lot before she could listen to two full songs.

"How did you beat me here?" Denise asked Terri once she parked and got out of the truck.

"I was at Southern Park Mall walking through Macy's when I called you."

"That new color and cut is bad, girl," Denise said as she examined Terri's head. "What made you chop it into layers?"

"Just time to do something new. You know, I've never cut my hair." Terri smiled and tucked a piece behind her ear. For as long as Denise could remember, the girl always wore her hair the same exact way - bone straight, super long, and a part in the middle. It was one of the things Denise thought was beautiful about Terri but, at times, could make her look like a little bit of a plain Jane. For years, she tried to get her to do something different and switch up her style but she wasn't having it at all. And even when Denise decided to cut her hair short, Terri still wouldn't budge.

"How long it's been? Why haven't you told me? I would've gone to the salon with you."

"I got it cut last week," Terri replied.

"So, how is your father-in-law doing?" Terri asked as they walked into the spa and directly up to the receptionist's desk.

"He's much better. Came home a couple of days ago but has to go to rehab."

"That's good," Terri said as they were led to the area where they would be massaged.

"I'm glad he's pulling through."

"He's a strong man. I knew he would make it."

"Terri, I wouldn't have been able to live with myself if he would've passed. I know Randy and I would've been in divorce court for sure."

"You're crazy, girl." Terri laughed.

145

"I'm serious."

"So, what are your plans since Randy's gone?"

"Well, first and foremost, I'm going to relax. I can't even tell you how stressful it's been to live in a house with that much tension. I just plan on having fun this week."

"Does that include Tyrone?"

"You know I would be lying if I said no. So, for the record, I'm keeping my mouth shut."

"In that case, I'll take it as a yes," Terri concluded.

They spent the entire hour chatting and, by the time they finished, Denise was relaxed and ready. She hadn't felt so at ease since her birthday. She went straight home and to her room where she spread out on the bed then searched the numbers in her phone until she settled onto Tyrone's.

"Hey baby. What are you doing right now?" she asked as she turned on the fifty inch plasma screen mounted on the wall.

"Going through some documents for a new account."

"You're always working hard," Denise replied.

"I'm surprised to hear from you. Haven't called me in a couple weeks."

"I know. I apologize. Something kind of came up at home."

"Why now? I am kind of busy," Tyrone said while Denise could hear him rummaging through papers in the background.

"Don't be mad. I was calling to see if you wanted to go out to dinner tonight."

"Did you check with your husband first," Tyrone replied.

"Oh! Someone's really upset."

"This is not the time to be sarcastic, Denise. Why you want to go out to dinner all of a sudden? We've haven't seen each other in over two weeks."

"I thought it'd be a good day to make up for lost time. My husband is out of town."

"Really? Well, what do you have in mind?" The line grew silent.

"A few things. But, dinner first."

"I suppose I can stop what I'm doing."

"How do seven, at Rachel's, sound?"

"I'll see you tonight," he said.

"See you then." Denise smiled, knowing she had him where she wanted him - eating right out of the palm of her hand. So, at that point, she chose to rest up for the evening. She figured she would need it.

When she woke up, Denise decided to go over her in-laws' house. She hadn't seen Daddy Tate since he was released and wanted to check on him. She knew Alice would probably have something smart to say, as always, but prayed that the Lord would put a muzzle on her tongue long enough for her visit him a little while. She hadn't really said two words to Denise since the big argument. And, from the way she constantly eyeballed her, she knew Randy talked to his mother about it.

During the entire drive over, Denise hoped she wouldn't lose her cool. She wasn't in the mood to exchange comments or insults with a woman who could barely stand the sight of her. As Denise pulled onto their street, her stomach began to do flips. She made a mental note to grab a snack to tide her over until dinner. She parked her car in the driveway, walked to the front door and rang the doorbell. Knowing how Alice liked to make her wait, she prepared herself to stand as long it took her to answer.

"I'm surprised to see you," she said immediately upon opening the front door. "With my son out of town and all, I thought you'd be running the streets."

Denise ignored her and walked into the living room where Randy's younger brother played a game on Playstation.

"Hey Will. What's up?"

"Nothing much, sis. About to go out in a little while."

"Where to?"

"Dave and Buster's wit some of my friends."

"That's cool. Well, take this." Denise reached in her purse and pulled out two twenty dollar bills and handed them to him.

"Thanks. You give me more money than my brother does. He's stingy."

"Have fun tonight. If you need more, just call."

"Alright! Cool!"

"So, what brings you over, Denise?" Mama Tate asked as she crossed her arms and sat on the end of the couch.

"To see how Daddy Tate was doing."

"He's in there." Alice pointed.

Denise took that as her cue to dismiss herself from the woman's presence. As she walked to the den, she saw Randy Sr. sitting in the recliner flipping through channels. Denise smiled as she saw her father-in-law his favorite chair, like his usual self. She hadn't seen him look that good in awhile.

"Hey baby. What you doing here?" He reached up and gave Denise a hug.

"You know I had to check on you. How are you feeling?" Denise sat across from him on the loveseat.

"Much better. But, I can't go out and run no marathon no more."

"That's good to hear. Are you listening to your doctor?"

"I'm trying. Although you know it's hard to go from doing everything to nothing at all."

"I know what you mean," Denise replied. "They put me on complete bed rest when I pulled those muscles in my back."

"I remember."

"I just pray you are really listening and taking it easy."

"Don't you worry, I am. I promise."

"Is there anything you need me to do? Like run to the store and pick up something for you?"

"No, he has everything he needs," Mama Tate said as she walked into the room. However, Randy Sr. looked up at her and rolled his eyes then decided to speak anyway.

"Honey, I'm fine. But, I do remember Alice saying we were out of sugar and butter." He sat back in his recliner and folded his arms over his chest.

"I do. But, I was going to run to the store later."

"Don't worry, Ma. I was on my way to Giant Eagle to do a little grocery shopping myself. I can get it up for you." Denise put on her biggest smile.

"You don't have to."

"No, it's no problem. I'll go and I'll be right back." Denise stated as she moved toward the door. She figured the only way she could truly torture Alice was to be extremely nice. Watching her squirm was satisfaction enough.

She picked up the things they needed from the store and took them back. She returned with great joy in placing the items directly in Alice's hands because it forced the woman to show gratitude and at least, say something nice. The look on her face was priceless and Denise wished she could've snapped a picture to always remember the moment. Even though Denise knew she only said thank you because she had to, she still felt good it was something positive for a change. She liked going back and forth with Alice exchanging smart comments from time to time but also desired to see her nice side once in a while.

Denise left for the second time with a smile on her face. But, when she got into her car, she felt her stomach do flips again. She glanced down at her watch and since she had four hours until her date with Tyrone, she went to a McDonald's and ordered a Big Mac extra value meal. Once she ate and was back in her car, she put in Goapele's song *Closer* and decided to take the scenic route.

Driving pass Crandall Park caused her to reminisce on how she and Michelle played there after school when they were growing up. They did everything at that playground from ride their bikes up and down the hills, climb the jungle gym, and throw rocks in the creek. Denise even had her first kiss there. The boy was fourteen, therefore, much more mature and advanced than her twelve years. They called each other boyfriend and girlfriend and one day they met up at the park to kiss after they thought Michelle wasn't paying attention. However, she saw them then speed home on her bike and told their mother. As Denise passed by the tree where it happened, she decided to call her sister and kick around some old memories but got her voicemail so she attempted to leave a message yet was interrupted by a text from Randy.

Hey Baby. In Atlanta. On way to check in. Call you later. Love you.

Denise sent a reply, stating she loved him as well and put her cell phone back in her pocket. There was nothing or no one that would stand in the way of her spending some time with Tyrone. She was glad Randy finally decided to come around and act like he wasn't mad at her anymore. But, he wouldn't be able to stand in her way of her game plan either. She figured he was probably feeling guilty for treating her the way he did over the past couple of weeks, concluding that he overreacted in light of the emergency. Denise couldn't think of ever giving him a reason to believe otherwise, despite the truth, and that was the way she wanted to keep it.

When she arrived at home, she went straight upstairs to prepare for the night. After refreshing herself in the bathroom, she stepped into her walk-in closet. Her eyes glanced over the entire span of the space, small enough to be an impoverished children's room, in search of the perfect outfit. She wanted to wear something to set Tyrone's senses on fire and, if she was successful, they just might skip dinner all together. Eventually, she settled on a new Baby Phat jumpsuit. *Oh yeah! When he sees me in this, we'll be getting doggie bags for sure,* she thought, as she slipped into the curve-hugging outfit and smiled at her silhouette in the full length mirror. She loved the fact she could try on anything and it fit her right. She felt her stomach doing flips again as she put on her two-inch, strappy heels while it was the same feeling she experienced earlier. She paid it no mind, yet checked her watch and decided to leave for the restaurant.

By the time Denise pulled her car into the parking lot, the feeling in her stomach subsided but was also glad to see Tyrone had arrived because she was hungry and ready to eat. Denise parked her car in the closest space to the main entrance then glanced in the mirror quickly checking her appearance.

I'm too fine for just one man. It has to be a crime to be so beautiful, she thought.

"You look amazing," Tyrone said as he opened the door for her. She could smell his Joop cologne which sent a chill up her spine.

"Thank you. You look alright yourself," Denise said then laughed.

"I don't know if I should be offended or turned on."

"Whatever you want. It's your choice."

"So, I can have whatever I want?" Tyrone asked.

"I never said that. You know what I meant." Denise swatted Tyrone's arm with her clutch purse.

"Yeah I know, even if you don't want to say it." Tyrone and Denise linked up arm in arm and walked into the restaurant as if they were truly a couple. The hostess greeted them and Denise responded before she marked off a place on her sheet and picked up two menus. They followed her. And, just as Denise was about mention they

151

preferred to sit in the secluded part of the dining room, she noticed the woman led them in that direction.

"Here's your table. Your waitress will be right with you," she said. Tyrone nodded and waited for the hostess to walk away before he spoke again.

"Why don't we skip dinner and go back to my place. The way you look right now I don't know if I can wait that long."

"Under normal circumstances, I would. But, I'm starving. Besides, the night's young. Who knows where we'll end up." Denise stomach growled as she finished speaking and she continued talking as if she hadn't heard it.

"Was that your stomach sounding like that?"

"I told you I'm hungry."

"Excuse me," Tyrone called out to the waitress approaching their table. Denise folded up her menu and ordered grilled fish, mixed vegetables, and a baked potato while Tyrone ordered a T-bone steak with a sweet potato. He also ordered a bottle of wine.

"I must admit I was really mad at you for not calling me back," he resumed.

"I understand. But, there was so much going on at my house with my husband. I felt like that was the solution for the moment."

"Trouble in paradise, huh?" Tyrone asked then laughed in a sarcastic manner.

"My father-in-law had a heart attack while I was at your house and my husband was pissed because he couldn't reach me."

"Did he suspect anything?"

"Yes. He asked me if there was somebody else."

"And? What did you say?"

"What you think I said? I told him no!"

"What you tell him that for!"

"It's not time…"

"It is time to stop lying so he can finally know the truth," Tyrone stated.

"Know what truth?"

"About us!" he replied and she could feel her nostrils flaring and her blood pressure rising at the same time.

"Tell him what about us, Tyrone?" Denise asked as she leaned in closer.

"That we're going to be together. It's inevitable. The way I feel about you is real. I know you feel the same way about me. We're going to be together one way or another. I know we've talked about keeping our relationship under wraps, but it's coming to the point where it's harder and harder for me to hide the way I feel. Honestly, I don't know how much longer I can keep quiet," he said in the cool, calmest manner.

Denise opened up her mouth in an attempt to curse Tyrone out but started to sense the same feeling in her stomach from earlier. She held up her finger to put a freeze on their conversation then hurried off to the restroom. She barely made it to the toilet before she vomited everything she consumed that day. She already hated using public toilets because they weren't sanitary enough, so having to hug the bowl with her face almost touching the dirty water made her throw up even more. For fifteen minutes, she couldn't bring herself to move. Finally, after she felt like she wasn't going to vomit again, she got up and washed her face then rinsed her mouth out in the sink. She couldn't understand why she was so sick because she rarely got the flu. When she returned to the table, she couldn't mask the ill look on her face.

"Is everything okay?"

"No, I am not feeling good. I don't know if it's something I ate earlier or what, but I'm sick as a dog."

"Let me take care of the check and I'll drive you to my house so you can get some rest."

"No, I'll be able to drive home." Denise picked her keys out of her purse and put on her black leather jacket. Even though she was not feeling well, she still didn't forget what they were talking about and planned on speaking her mind once she felt better.

"Let me take care of you."

"It's okay, Tyrone. I can take care of myself. I'm going home. I'll call you in the morning," she uttered as she left him sitting at the table.

Chapter Fourteen

Denise remained sick the entire time Randy was away. She threw up then grew dizzy and light headed almost everyday since going to dinner with Tyrone. Her sudden illness caused her to cancel her plans and, once Randy got back in town, she went back to not talking to or contacting Tyrone at all. She knew he was angry because he called and sent texts, but she didn't return or respond to any of his messages. She wanted to talk to Tyrone and at least see how he was doing but couldn't run the risk of getting caught. Randy had already been on her heels and she couldn't afford to be caught this late in the game. There was a part of her that felt bad about ignoring Tyrone but another told her she had to do whatever it took to keep her marriage together. He knew what he signed up for when they got involved. And, if he wanted to continue seeing her, he had to be content with the conditions of her relationship, she reasoned as she sat in church watching her husband in deliver his sermon.

"Whom the Son sets free, is free indeed," Randy preached then members of his congregation agreed by saying, "Amen." Denise clapped and praised as looked at her husband, knowing he was an excellent pastor and Oakdale Baptist should be proud to have him. Then, she sat back in the pew and thought about the first time they met...

She worked at JC Penny's as a sales associate and he walked through her section of the store one day. Upon noticing Denise, he stopped and started talking to her. He said he had never seen her in there before and asked if she was from out of town. She told him she grew up in the city all her life and they realized they knew some of the same people. Randy was immediately drawn to her breathtaking appearance while Denise was attracted to his appearance as well as the way he carried himself. From talking to Randy, she knew there was something different about him and there was no doubt she wanted to see him again. He ended up inviting her to the church he attended but Denise was reluctant. She wasn't really fond of worshipping after her experiences with her father. However, Randy was so fine she would've become a nun just to get next to him.

Before then, she hadn't been to a church service for a couple of years. She was a member of her father's and used to love going with him, her mother, and sister. It made her feel as if they had the perfect family and nothing could mess until up his infidelities surfaced, causing people to start talking as well as staring. It changed her life as she knew it. Her parents' divorce forced him to resign as senior pastor and their family was torn apart. They were still welcome to be apart of the congregation, but her mother was embarrassed to the point that they stopped going all together.

Denise was so hurt that she vowed to never go to church or trust another man again. She couldn't stand what her father did to their family and she hated him for it. Even though he supposedly changed his ways and stopped sleeping around with women, she still didn't care for him. As far as she was concerned, he was just the man who contributed his sperm to create her and nothing more. Her sister Michelle had a different view on the whole situation. She was furious to learn of the affair and didn't speak to him for a long time afterwards. They ended up reconciling a few years later while she was away at college. Michelle kept in touch with him. Denise didn't want anything to do with him. The only reason he had her current phone number was because Michelle had given it to him. Otherwise, he wouldn't have known it at all.

So, when Randy told her he was in training to become a minister, she pulled away for a long while. Hearing his passion about it brought back too many familiar feelings and she wondered if she could trust him. What her father did made her look at people in ministry differently. She began to see so many claiming to be of the cloth and preaching one thing while living a completely different way. When it came to Randy, she questioned what would make him any different than the rest. For a while, she considered him to be just a friend. But, she also couldn't fight her feelings. It seemed like the more she tried, the more she fell deeper and deeper in love. He was so sweet and always doing things to make her feel special. She put her guard up and expected for him to be a jerk at any moment. But, surprisingly, that never happened.

He was the perfect gentleman and never did anything to cause discomfort, definitely different than the guys she was used to dating. Denise decided she wanted to wait until marriage to have sex. And when she was with Randy, he never pressured her because he was saving himself as well. So, as she weighed the pros and cons of being in a relationship with preacher, she determined the good outweighed the bad and decided to really allow herself to love him. They dated for almost two years and she managed to keep her painful past a secret from Randy until it was forced to rear its ugly head.

Randy had really fallen in love, as well, and decided he would propose on Christmas Eve at her mom's house. When he popped the question, he expected Denise to jump up and down then say yes. But, she did the

157

opposite. Instead, she burst into tears and ran outside. He ran after her but they got into a huge argument which caused them to break up. If it wasn't for Michelle calling Randy to tell her the real reason behind Denise's response, he would not have returned. However, he tracked Denise called and forced her to talk to him. She mentioned her father's infidelity and how she was scared to trust, that he would do the same thing to her if they got married.

Randy cried at Denise's confession and vowed to never hurt her if she honestly gave him a chance. And for their entire marriage, he made sure to stay true to his word. He didn't even converse with women unless someone else was present while that was just one of the many things he promised so he wouldn't be put in that predicament. She knew she had a faithful husband who has never given her a reason to think otherwise but she also knew all it took was the right one to make her husband fall. She trusted him but he was still a man. And, if given the right opportunity with little to no repercussion, he would seize take advantage of it, she thought...

Denise refocused her attention to Randy as he finished up his sermon. She stared into his eyes. Then, he winked and smiled before walking down from the pulpit toward the pew. Automatically, Denise grabbed Randy's hand to join in front of the church.

"Now, here is the part of the service I always love because I get to come down and be with my beautiful wife and bring new people into our family," Randy said as he gave the microphone to Denise and kissed her on her cheek. She smiled from ear to ear as she straightened her gray pinstripe skirt.

"If anyone doesn't have a church home, we want you to know that the doors of Oakdale Baptist are open. So, if you would like to join us, please come up and do so at this time," Denise stated while the organist played an inviting tune and Randy held out their arms at the same time as if they had practiced the gesture over and over. A woman with two small children made her way to the front then two teenage girls came forward in front of a tall dark-skinned man. As he got closer to the front of the sanctuary, Denise thought she was having a bad dream.

She tried her best to maintain composure since the last thing she needed was to lose control. It was the moment where she would either pass or fail and she most definitely wanted to succeed. She looked straight ahead as if she didn't see him then Randy handed the microphone to the new members so they could say their names before Denise blessed and received them. Usually, she didn't mind welcoming the joining members. It actually made her very happy because it equaled more money. However, this time was different while she couldn't believe what was taking place right before her eyes. And regardless of what went on, she was determined to not act like a fool. There was no way she was going to embarrass herself in front of three thousand people.

As the music continued, the church clapped in unison. Soon after, Randy dismissed everyone from service. The entire church lined the center aisle to greet the members while Denise got in the front of the line and hugged the single mother, teenage girls, and then Tyrone. With the way he grinned, you would've thought he just won the lottery. Denise wanted to slap the hell out of him but at the front of the altar was not the appropriate place. Instead, she promised to deal with him later then put on her best smile.

"God bless you," Denise uttered as they embraced. She smelled her favorite cologne on him. As she let go, Tyrone whispered in her ear.

"I love you," he said. Randy stood almost directly behind Denise in the greeting line, which left her no time to even whisper a few choice words back. She tried to continue walking back to her seat for her purse. But, before she could get away, Randy held onto her hand.

"Blessing, Brother Tyrone. We're so glad you decided to join this ministry,"
Randy said they shook hands.

"Thank you for allowing me to be a part of your church. I was a little undecided. But, from the moment I stepped foot inside, I knew it was where I should be." He grinned so hard it seem like he was bound to pop a blood vessel.

"I know you already met her but I want to introduce you to my wife. This is my first lady, Denise Tate," Randy continued. Denise forced a tight smirk on her face and shook his hand.

"Hello, Denise. It's nice to meet you. You know, pastor, my girlfriend's name is Denise and she has short hair too." Tyrone winked at her.

"Really? What a coincidence? Well, I hope you invite her to come with you as well and feel free to become involved. We encourage it," Randy said as Denise tugged on his arm, signaling she was ready to go.

"Thank you, Pastor Tate. And I will definitely do that," Tyrone mentioned before he started moving to the exit. Naively, Randy squeezed her hand and smiled.

"Nice, brother," he said as they began to walk away as well before preparing to go home. When they got in the car, they engaged in idle chat as drove.

"All I have to do is warm the food when we get home," Denise said while staring out of the window and considering the actions of Tyrone.

"Did you get a chance to invite everyone over for dinner today?" Randy asked as he turned into their housing development.

"Yes," she responded, then rattled off the guest list, which included her own mother and step-father.

"You invited my mother?" Randy asked, looking surprised. "Oh, Denise, I forgot to grab some pop from the store so I'll be right back." He pulled in their driveway let her get out and drove off.

Once in the house, she sat her Bible and her purse on the dining room chair. Then, the phone rang as she attempted to go upstairs. She turned around to answer it and after picking up the receiver, saw Terri's number on display.

"Just the person I need to talk to... You still coming over? Aren't you?"

"Actually, I'm on the front porch. Can't you hear you bell ringing."

"No. But, good because we need to talk." She went to the door and unlocked it then Terri walk in. Denise didn't even give her a chance to talk before she started telling her what happened to her in church.

"You've got to be kidding me?"

"I wish I was."

"So are you going to keep seeing him?"

"Ever since Randy has been back from Atlanta, I haven't been talking to anyone. That's why he did what he did."

"I see... You think he would come out about your relationship?"

"Honestly, at this point, I don't know. I never thought he would step foot in the church. And, he joined today so anything's possible."

"I told you that man was crazy."

"Now, I'm beginning to see exactly what you mean. I thought it was fun at first."

"What I'm saying is you need to end it before this whole thing comes back and blows up in your face."

"I know but, with Tyrone a member, I don't know what to do."

"If I were you, I would just put an end to it all. Things already out of control. You don't want it to get any worse."

The friends talked for twenty more minutes until the other guests started to arrive. Denise told her they would have to resume the conversation later as she opened up the door for the deacon and his wife. After greeting them, she took both of their coats and hung them in the hallway closet. The deacon held a blue and white casserole dish in his hand, so Denise pointed him in the direction of the kitchen.

"What have you made for us to eat this Sunday?" he asked as he returned then started to rub his stomach and smile.

"I made a little bit of everything," said Denise. "Smothered pork chops, barbecue chicken, collard greens, mash potatoes, candied yams, salad, and corn pudding."

"Oh my goodness! Well, I can't wait to eat." He laughed.

"Now, I want to know what was in that casserole dish," she continued.

"I made some of my sweet and cheesy macaroni and cheese," his wife replied.

"Well, I hope you know I'm going to put that up and save it for me," Denise warned.

"Don't worry, I'll make you some and bring it to church on Wednesday," the deacon's wife responded before being interrupted by a female voice.

"Where's my favorite sister at?" Michelle stated while walking through the door.

"I'm your only sister." Denise walked up and hugged her then they both started chuckling but her laughter seized when Jimmy entered. It took everything within her not to say something. Michelle could feel her sister on the verge spitting venom, so she immediately started talking.

"Denise, you got a shirt I can wear? I spilled some juice on mine."

"Come with me upstairs." Denise walked past Jimmy and didn't say a word while her sister followed.

"I already know what you're thinking," Michelle uttered when she walked in Denise's bedroom and shut the door.

"So, when did this happen?" Denise faced Michelle and crossed her arms.

"A lot has happened since the last time we talked."

"I see... You let him come back."

"Denise, I didn't plan on it... It just happened. Besides, he's really changed."

"How do you know that? He's only been gone for like two months," Denise said sarcastically.

"I know. But, in that time, he started working another job and is making some good money. He's stopped drinking and is going to church."

"What church? He hasn't been coming to our church. I'm sorry, Michelle, but doesn't he always do this when he's trying to come back?"

"Yes. But, I can really see the difference this time. He's been going to the church where he attends alcoholic's anonymous meetings. And he's my husband. I'm not trying to give up on him that easily."

"Okay Michelle, I'm not going to say anything else when he ends up hurting you. Just say, I told you so."

"I know you're concerned but I'm trying to make things work."

"I perfectly understand and I respect your decision. Here. Let's hurry up and go downstairs because I can hear everybody's here," Denise replied as she handed her a blouse out of one of her drawers. She didn't know why it surprised her to see Jimmy with her sister and the kids. Throughout the years of their marriage, he always left then turned right around and came back. Every time, Michelle swore up and down she wasn't going to surrender but somehow it always happened.

When they went back downstairs, Denise saw Jimmy's face first and he smiled at her as if he tried to irritate her nerves, so she rolled her eyes right before they prayed.

"Lord, we thank you for this food. Let it be nourishing to our bodies. In Jesus name. Amen."

"Amen," everyone else repeated after Randy said the blessing.

"This food smells delicious." The deacon picked up his plate and started to fill it up with chicken.

"I know the food tastes good because she can cook," Jimmy replied and Denise bit her lip to keep from making a comment.

"Denise, this food tastes really good." Mama Tate laughed as she shoved a forkful of candied yams in her mouth.

"Thanks Alice." She smiled and Randy winked at her. Denise didn't know why she tried to be friendly, thought she was maybe attempting to turn over a new leaf. Moreover, Denise didn't care. She was just glad they were getting along. "Well, I'll be the first to say I am so glad my father-in-law is on his feet."

"I'm glad, baby. You know I was going to come, especially since you're cooking."

"Where did you learn to cook like that?" the deacon asked as he licked the last traces of BBQ sauce from his fork. Before Denise got a chance to answer, Randy spoke.

"She got it from her mama." The whole room went up in laughter as he began to make a song and dance to his own beat. Denise's mother smiled.

"Randy you are so crazy," she replied as she laughed.

"I'm glad you liked the food, deacon," Randy said then he signaled for Denise to leave the room with him. They slipped away from the dining room and walked into Randy's office.

"What's up baby?" Denise smiled as Randy shut the door.

"I wanted to talk to you, alone," he said as he walked over to the chaise lounge and sat on the edge while she took a seat on the couch.

"What's on your mind?" she asked.

"I just wanted to tell you I'm glad things are getting better between us I am sorry I accused you of stepping out on me. I know you've been working hard at making things work between us so I have a surprise for you." Randy pulled a brown envelope out of his jacket pocket and reached over to give it to Denise.

"What's this?" She held it in her hands.

"A trip to Jamaica," he continued. With much excitement, she moved toward him to show her gratitude. "I know how much you love Jamaica. We had so much fun the last time, so I decided to take you back for our anniversary."

"Randy, I'm so happy."

"I love you, baby," he said. Denise smiled from ear to ear as they rejoined their family in the dining room. She then asked Terri to follow her to the kitchen and help bring the punch so she could tell her the news.

"Guess what Randy just told me?"

"It must be something good by your ridiculous smile," Terri responded before Denise revealed her anniversary plans. "Girl, I am so jealous. I can't believe he's taking you there again. And, didn't he take you to Turks and Caicos, too?" she inquired as she removed the punch bowl out from the fridge then placed it on the table.

"Yeah. And, it was the bomb. We even stayed at the Sandal's Resort and were treated like celebrities."

"I'm not mad at you. I just can't wait until I get a hold of a man that will do those kinds of things for me." Terri pulled a chair out and sat down.

"Don't worry. You will. But, you know he also has to make more money than you and you already earn a grip." Denise leaned on the counter.

"You know what. That's how I used to think. Shoot. That was my first requirement coming through the door. But now, as long as he makes a decent income and treats me like a queen. That's all I need."

"Seems like you've relaxed your standards a little bit."

"Being alone on many a night will do that to you."

"What happened to that guy you was seeing that was a lawyer too?"

"Let me see. How I want to put this since it is Sunday and I don't want to curse. Well, to put it lightly, he was a straight hoe. Trying to sleep with all of the female colleagues in the office, including me. So, I had to kick him to the curb. I'm sorry but I need a man that is little bit old fashioned, you know. Don't be trying to get my loving and everybody else's, too."

"I feel you."

"I wasn't expecting to see Jimmy today. I thought you told me that they were separated."

"That was the impression I was under too until he showed up today. I haven't talked to my sister in a while so I didn't know he had come back home. But, I don't think she'd run tell me the news either."

"Why you say that?"

"Because, she know that I can't stand him and the advice I gave is to leave that man alone. He is a dog and is doing nothing but dragging her and the kids down."

"I understand. But, that is her husband. You got to give her credit for at least trying to make everything work instead of running and getting a divorce."

"Yeah, but what is she gonna do when he does the same thing to her? Who is she gonna run to when he starts back drinking and decides to step out on her again. Me. And I'll be telling her the same old thing I always say. Leave that man alone and move on."

"Yeah, but that's her decision not yours. She'll be alright 'cause your sister is a strong woman."

"You're right. She is. But, if Jimmy hurts her again, I will hurt him."

"Okay, I still see you like to fight." Terri laughed.

Denise looked around to see if Randy was anywhere near and then she heard him upstairs shutting their bedroom door so she decided to continue their conversation from earlier.

"Terri, when I saw Tyrone strut down that center aisle all big bad and bold I didn't know what to think," she whispered.

"If I was in your situation, I probably would've peed on myself right there in front of everybody. Tyrone is crazy."

"Tell me about it."

"Just make sure you keep your eyes open and watch him for real. Because if he was brave enough to join your church, there ain't no telling what he will do next if he's pushed to that point."

Terri and Denise brought the punch out and set the Waterford Crystal bowl before everyone. They jumped right back into the conversation at the dinner table where the deacon talked about how some of the young people at the church dress, but Denise's mind seemed to be elsewhere. She thought about what her friend said. *If he was bold enough to join your church, then God knows what he'll do next.* That statement really started to bother her because she knew it was the truth. She tried to move on and think about other things like her upcoming vacation and her marriage but those words still managed to replay over and over in her mind.

"Baby, our dinner turned out nice didn't it?" Randy asked as they waved goodbye to everyone walking to their car at the end of their circular driveway.

"Yes it did. I love it when we all get together." Denise closed the door and locked it. When she turned around Randy was directly in front of her and had his arms stretched out. She walked up to him and became lost in his warm embrace.

"Honey, I want to say I'm sorry about how I acted during the time when Dad had the heart attack. It was wrong of me and I apologize."

"Babe, you don't have to. I understand what you were going through and I'm sorry for not being there for you like I'm supposed to. So, please forgive me." Randy leaned down and planted a kiss on her lips. She smiled and kissed him back. She couldn't wait to take the vacation. At this point she considered it to be long overdue.

Randy held Denise in his embrace and she couldn't help but smile. It felt so good to be in his arms again. So good, Denise wished it wouldn't end but their hug was interrupted by a ringing phone. She heard it but ignored it, figuring that whoever could wait. But Randy didn't overlook the beeping.

"Denise, is that your phone?" he asked.

"I think so. Let me go and get it." Denise walked down the hallway to the kitchen where it sat on the counter top. She picked it up and the screen flashed.

I BET YOU WON'T EVER GO WITHOUT TALKING TO ME AGAIN. HAVE A GOOD NIGHT.

Denise deleted the message and put her phone down as Randy walked into the kitchen and asked, "Who was that, babe?"

"Oh, it was Terri. She wants to know if I'm free for lunch tomorrow. Forgot to ask while she was here, I guess," Denise explained as she placed the phone back onto the counter then took her husband's hand to lead him upstairs.

"Oh okay," Randy answered as he followed with both of them anticipating a fairy tale ending on that evening and beyond, until parted by death.

Chapter Fifteen

Denise looked over at the alarm clock and realized it was close to noon. Normally, she would've been out of bed at eight o'clock but, on this day, she could barely move. She attempted to get up and going but, every time she tried, she ended up hanging over the side vomiting in a trash can. Some of the church members were starting to come down with the flu and, although she had the symptoms, she didn't think that to be her diagnosis as a lot of changes occurred in her body lately. She was sick only in the mornings, the smell of favorite foods made her nauseas, her breasts were sensitive, and her regular jeans didn't fit. Her period failed to come for two months in a row and, even though she knew of many women whose monthly cycles were irregular, she believed she was pregnant. She had picked up a pregnancy test while out shoe shopping the day before and was ready to find out if her suspicions were true indeed.

Denise managed to get out of bed and slowly walked into the bathroom. She removed the test from its hiding spot underneath the sink, opened it, read the instructions, and followed them exactly before sitting on the edge of the tub to wait for the results. When she saw the line indicating she was with child, she felt the nauseous feeling return all over again. And by the time

Randy came home for lunch, she laid in the same spot she was in when he left.

"Denise, are you okay," he said while entering the bedroom.

"I've been sick all morning. It feels like, if I try to move, I'll throw up."

Randy went into the bathroom and returned with a thermometer then stuck it in Denise's mouth. He waited for it to beep then examined the reading.

"You don't have a fever," Randy said.

"I feel horrible."

"Well, I came home before my next meeting so that I could see about you."

"Babe, you didn't have to. I'll be fine. All I need is some Ginger Ale. You can go back to work. I'll be okay."

"Are you sure? I can cancel my plans."

"No, honey."

"Okay. But, if you need me, please call. I can come back to help you feel better." Randy kissed Denise on her forehead.

After Randy left, she tried to get up but she could barely move so she decided to just sleep for the rest of the day until she was awakened by the ringing her house phone. When she looked at the caller I.D., she saw a private number.

"Praise the Lord. Tate residence," she managed to mumble.

"It feels so good to hear your voice," Tyrone said.

"What are you doing dialing this number?"

"I know. But I really missed you and wanted to hear your voice."

"So, you call my home?"

"I couldn't help myself," he continued.

"You've been unable to help yourself a lot lately. I still can't believe you came to my husband's church."

"Why? Everyone comes to a point in their life when they need a change. I feel like this was my time."

"Cut the crap. You know you didn't join for that reason."

"So, I take it, you're not happy about it?"

"Oh, can you tell?"

"I thought it would be a good idea if we worshipped together. We already do everything else."

"You know you crossed the line. I don't even know why I'm having this conversation with you. Goodbye," Denise replied and ended the call. Tyrone's phone call stressed her out to the point of a headache. All she had the strength to do was be still. She drifted off to sleep and was awaken by Randy stroking her face.

"Hey baby, I ended up canceling one of my counseling sessions to come back and check on you," he said as he sat on the edge of the bed next to her.

"Honey, you didn't have to do that. I've been resting." Denise yawned and stretched her arms over her head.

"How do you feel? Are you up to going to dinner with your sister and Jimmy? I'll cancel." Randy asked.

"No, I'll be fine by tonight. I just need to stay in bed for a little while longer," Denise answered and gave him a quick kiss before dropping her head back on the pillow.

The extra time she spent in bed proved to be what she needed. Denise was able to get herself up and dressed in no time. Glad she was feeling better so she could go to dinner with her sister, she decided on wearing a black dress. She didn't care to see her brother-in law Jimmy. However, she made a promised to herself to not say anything out of the way unless he said something crazy to her. Then, she wouldn't be responsible for what might occur.

As Randy drove them to the restaurant, Denise couldn't help but stare out the window. She had a lot on her mind. Finding out she was pregnant put her mindset in another place. She couldn't even seem to concentrate on the conversation her husband tried to have with her.

"Hey babe, is everything okay? Looks like something on your mind," Randy said as he glanced over at Denise still stared out the window.

"No. Nothing's on my mind. What makes you think that?" Denise turned her head and attention toward him.

"Just looks that way. That's all."

"No, I'm fine. Just a little hungry since I haven't ate all day," she continued as Randy pulled into the lot and parked right next to Jimmy and Michelle's Silver Honda Accord.

When they entered the building, Denise saw them sitting off in a corner booth. When Jimmy noticed them walking toward their table, he started smiling at Denise like she would be happy to see him but she rolled her eyes and smoothed her dress to make sure her tiny bump wasn't visible.

"We're glad you could join us," Jimmy said as they sat down across from each other.

"We're happy to celebrate your new promotion." Randy nodded his head at Jimmy and Michelle shook her head in agreement.

"What can I say? God is good. He has definitely been working in my life. I'm just thankful for his blessings. That's all," Jimmy replied. Denise didn't paying attention. She had her menu pulled up in front of her face, hoping he would understand she wasn't interested in anything he had to say and he would shut up.

"Baby. Is everything okay? You're awfully quiet," Randy asked. Denise lowered the menu just enough to see her husband.

"I'm okay. I don't know what I want to eat though. I'm extremely hungry," she continued, getting tired of trying to pretend to like her brother-in-law while Randy wasn't making the situation any better with his attempts to make her a part of the conversation when it was clear she didn't want to participate.

"Denise, where did you buy that dress? It looks great on you." Michelle tried to shift the conversation in another direction.

"Oh, I picked this up from Macy's about three months ago." Denise put down her menu and smiled at her sister.

"You look great, sis," Jimmy replied.

Denise grew annoyed by Jimmy insistence upon trying to say something to her so she ignored his comment. Randy cut Denise a look for not acknowledging him, but couldn't address it because the waitress came and took their orders. As soon she left their table, Randy turned to Denise.

"Babe, Jimmy complimented you on how nice you look."

"Oh, you were talking to me?" Denise asked, trying to play aloof.

"Yeah honey, I'm pretty sure you're his only sister at the table."

"Thanks Jimmy," she answered through clenched teeth.

"You're more than welcome. Just glad we're kid free and have the whole weekend to ourselves," he replied as he winked at Michelle.

Denise wanted to scream at him trying so hard to be romantic with her sister. She knew he was a dog from the first time she met him and was determined to make her sister see her husband for what he truly was, a FAKE. Jimmy never made an effort to compliment Michelle, take her out, or even show public affection. So, she just knew he was being fraudulent and acting like a lust-driven, crazed teenager.

"Excuse me for a moment, I have to take this call," Randy mentioned as he looked at his ringing cell phone then got up from the table.

"I have to use the restroom. I'll be right back," Michelle said while she got up. Denise wished she had a reason to excuse herself but the waitress brought their dinner to them so she knew that was the perfect excuse to not say anything to him.

"Are you enjoying your dinner?" Jimmy asked. Denise stuffed her mouth so she wouldn't have to speak. She hoped he got the hint and would shut up but he didn't.

"Denise, are you okay? Seems like you've had an attitude the entire time we've here. And, if I didn't know any better, it appears to be with me."

"Alright look, Jimmy. Since you want me to talk to you, I'ma get straight to the point. You've been acting like Mr. Romance with you're newest, self-proclaimed change but I see straight through you."

"Oh. And, what is it that you see?" Jimmy raised his eyebrows and his nostrils flared.

"You're nothing but a dog and I've been doing my best not to say anything to you out of respect for my sister and nephews but I can't take it no more."

"You can't take what no more," he asked.

"You're acting like you're all in love with my sister when I know you haven't changed one bit. You're still the same Jimmy from when I first met you."

"I don't know how many times I have to tell you I have changed, I am a different man from the way I was before and…" he attempted to explain before she cut him off.

"Look, don't preach your sermon to me. All I'm saying is you better be doing right by my sister and my nephews or else." She leaned up on the table and crossed her arms.

"Or else what?" he asked.

"It would be very hard for me to explain to my nephews that their daddy died of natural causes and went to heaven. Now, wouldn't it?" She stared at Jimmy in his face.

"Are you threatening me?"

"Oh, it's definitely a threat. Don't try me," Denise added, wanting Jimmy to know that if he even thought about causing her sister any more problems, he wouldn't live to make things right. She was tired of Jimmy thinking he could get away with it his behaviors while she experienced, first-hand, the pain Michelle felt when he left. She wasn't trying to go through that again. She believed Michelle was a good woman who didn't deserve someone like him. But, since she decided to stay with Jimmy and work things out, Denise felt forced to take matters into her own hands. He was about to speak but Randy and Michelle returned while they all tried to enjoy the rest of the evening.

Three days later, Denise called her sister to see what she was doing and, since she had the day off, they decided to meet for lunch. They sat across from each other at Panera Bread. Then, as soon as they received their food, Denise told Michelle she had something important to discuss, took a deep breath, and went for it.

"What? Are you serious? This is big news. Have you went to the doctor? How far along you are?"

"No. Not yet. I just took a pregnancy test about four days ago."

"What are you waiting on?" Michelle asked.

"Nothing… I just haven't gone yet."

"That doesn't mean anything. You still need to go." Michelle looked down at Denise stomach and pointed.

"I thought I noticed a little pouch in your otherwise flat stomach."

"Initially, I thought it was because I haven't been working out…"

"I'm surprised Randy hasn't noticed. But you need to make an appointment with my doctor so you can at least find out your due date."

"I know. I'm just shocked. I never thought Randy and I would have kids."

"I knew it would happen someday. Besides, Randy's wanted you to get pregnant since you said I do. I know you may be a little nervous because you don't know what to expect but you'll be fine."

"Guess I'll make an appointment with Dr. Lovett when I come back from Jamaica next week."

"Does Randy even know that you may possibly be pregnant?" Michelle continued then Denise eyes grew big.

"No, and I want to keep it that way until the doctor tells me for sure."

"Whatever Denise. I just better be the first person to know," she stated as the finished their meal.

Denise tried to act like she wasn't one-hundred percent sure but, after the pregnancy test, she was certain. Besides Michelle, Denise planned on telling Terri the news but that was about it. She wasn't excited at all because having a baby would alter her life and she didn't know if she wanted it to change so drastically. Ever since she found out, she was in her own little world. She had become withdrawn to the point that Randy was worried about her but she convinced him there was nothing wrong.

After she left with her sister, she pulled up in the driveway and saw Tyrone's white Lincoln Navigator parked next to Randy's Cadillac. She almost put her car in reverse to leave but had to use the bathroom and felt like she wouldn't make it if she tried to go somewhere else. She wasn't even surprised Tyrone was at their home because, as of late, he seemed to pop up everywhere as he became a devoted member of Oakdale. He attended every Sunday service, Tuesday night Bible study, Thursday choir rehearsals, and Friday night prayer meetings since he joined a month prior. She tried to do her best to act as if she didn't know him but was forced to see him almost everyday. With all that in mind, she cringed as she entered the house knowing he was there as well.

"Hey baby. I didn't even hear you come in," Randy said as he got up from his desk and kissed Denise.

"I had to park at the end of the driveway because your cars are blocking the garage." Denise smiled.

"Oh! I'm sorry, honey. Give me your keys and I'll move mine. You remember Brother Tyrone, don't you?" Randy continued while Denise handed him her keys.

"How are you, Sister Denise? It's so good to see you again." Tyrone stood up and shook her hand. He did wait for Randy to leave before he tried to speak again but Denise didn't give him the opportunity.

"So, you're trying to be my husband's best friend now?"

"We discussing some things we're going to be doing with the men's ministry this year. Is that alright with you, Sister Tate?"

"Unbelievable!"

"And I decided to meet him here, instead of the church, because I missed you."

"If you that's the case, then all you had to do was call. Not show up at my house!"

"You know you don't like to return phone calls sometimes. So, I gotta do what I gotta do," he taunted. Just as Denise opened up her mouth to say something else, Randy came back in the house.

"Like I was saying, your husband and I came up with plans for the men..."

"Brother Tyrone, you know I can't take any of the credit for what we talked about. They were all your ideas. Baby, Tyrone wants to do some wonderful things. I'm glad he's the new leader of that ministry."

With all of the extracurricular activities he so willingly joined, Denise facetiously thought it was only a matter of time before he pretended to be called to preaching.

"Well, Pastor Tate, I didn't mean to take up all your time. I just wanted to share the things that's been on my heart."

"It's perfectly fine, Tyrone. I like when people want to be involved. It makes my job a lot easier." Randy chuckled.

"I'll get going. Probably call your cell phone tomorrow. We can discuss getting these activities going. Nice to see you again, Sister Denise."

"You too." She smiled, exposing clenched teeth.

"God Bless you, brother. Talk to you tomorrow."

"Baby, can you let Tyrone out please?" Randy asked.

"Sure." Denise blinked several times to help her think as she answered her husband. She had the urge to knock Tyrone upside his head with one of the glass vases sitting on Randy's desk but resisted the temptation. Instead, she walked toward the exit and opened it. She couldn't wait for Tyrone to walk his slimy, conniving self out of their home but he stopped in the doorway.

"Can I get a goodbye kiss," Tyrone whispered in Denise's ear.

"You are going too far," she uttered but, before she could say anything else, his tongue traveled from her ear to her lips where he quickly pressed them. She swiftly jerked away.

"You are crazy," she whispered back to him and looked back to see if Randy had come out of his office.

"If you think I am crazy now, you haven't seen nothing yet," Tyrone replied and walked away. She shut the door, locked it, and went into the powder room where she rinsed her mouth off.

Denise heard Tyrone start up his car and pull off as she came out of the bathroom and saw Randy. "So, how did Brother Tyrone end up over here? I thought you said you didn't want too many people from the congregation knowing where we lived?" she asked.

"I know, babe. I didn't plan on it. Just happened. We were going to meet at the church but I started to get tired so I told him we could set our meeting for a later date. But he insisted on us meeting and offered to drop by."

"How did he know where we lived? You know someone is always getting lost when coming out here," Denise asked as she sat in one of his black leather chairs. She felt a lump form in the middle of her throat.

"I thought I would have to explain it to him. But when I told him where we lived, he said he already knew the way because he had a friend who lived in this neighborhood."

"Oh," she responded.

"Yes. He told me he would like for me to meet her sometime. I really like Tyrone. He has a real hunger for the things of God and helping our ministry. Glad God sent him our way," Randy continued.

Denise tried not to have an attitude while he sang Tyrone's praises because she knew her husband was being truly sincere about how he felt about him. But, she knew that man didn't have a hunger for anything that had to do with God. He was only concerned with religion because it involved her and was trying to do whatever he could to tear down everything she'd worked so hard to keep in her life.

"Well, I don't mean to be rude and change the subject or anything, but I'm glad God sent you my way." Denise wrapped her arms around her husband and kissed him passionately.

"Me too."

"I'm even happier we're getting ready to go on vacation. We need to get away."

"Yes, we do."

Denise smiled as she thought about her impending vacation with her husband and, even though Tyrone did everything he could to be a road block in her life, she planned to put everything aside and enjoy herself before coming back home to rid Tyrone from her life and make decisions about the one growing inside of her stomach.

Chapter Sixteen

Despite feeling sick in the cab ride to the airport and nearly vomiting in the ladies room while Randy checked their luggage, the plane ride to Jamaica was surprisingly smooth for Denise. She was able to keep down the turkey sandwich and plain potato chips the flight attendants served but slept the majority of the trip.

"Baby, we're landing wake up," Randy whispered as he tapped her arm.

"How long have I been sleep?" She rubbed her eyes then reached inside her purse for her compact while he put away the latest issue of Gospel Today magazine.

"The entire time. I didn't want to wake you."

"I'm feeling good." She smiled.

"Well, you're looking better," Randy responded before kissing Denise.

"Baby, don't lie. I know I look a mess." She giggled.

"I'm not. Denise Tate, you're the most beautiful woman in the world," he continued since he always complimented her no matter how she appeared.

The plane landed and, eventually, Denise and Randy exited then grabbed their luggage before walking to their designated gate. There, they saw a man standing and holding a white sign with their name on it. Once they approached him, he greeted them then introduced himself with a strong Jamaican accent. Tall with dark chocolate skin and shoulder-length dreads pulled back in a ponytail, he had to be one of the most beautiful Jamaican men Denise had ever seen as she was mesmerized by his sweet physique from the moment she laid eyes on him. He had a body most men die for and wore a blue shirt, open to reveal abs that would make one want to wash their clothes on them. The driver carried their bags to the Suzuki Jeep and Randy helped him load them into the truck before they climbed in. He put his arm around her and looked out of the window at the beautiful scenery while riding through the countryside. After about twenty minutes, the driver pulled up to property occupied with nothing but small homes. They got out, the men unloaded, and all proceed into one of the private villas.

"If you need anything, dial my office. I'll be here right away." The driver pointed to the phone sitting on the wicker coffee table.

"Thanks," Denise said as he headed to the door then left.

"That guy was very nice." Randy smiled.

"Yeah, he was," Denise said as she took two of her Louis Vuitton suitcases and put them in the spacious master bedroom located at the end of the hallway. Randy tiptoed behind her and grabbed her from behind.

"Now, we're finally alone. No cell phones, pagers, Oakdale, prayer requests. It's just you and me," he explained then Denise turned around and met his lips for all conversation to stop as they enjoyed each other's presence.

Denise and Randy made their way to a chaise lounge positioned in the corner of the room, right next to the bed. She didn't say a word as they removed their clothes so he could kiss every nook and cranny of her body.

"I know it gets rough having to share me, but I wanted to take you on this vacation to show you how much I really appreciate you."

"I appreciate you too, baby," Denise replied.

"No, I really, really appreciate you from the bottom of my heart." Randy began to shower her with kisses all over and the sensation from his lips sent an electric shock up and down her spine.

Denise was never the type of woman who would leave a man hanging, so she proceeded to do everything she could think of to bring her husband pleasure. And, both knew good and well they were on vacation and should be sightseeing, but all things had to wait because it was the time for them to enjoy each other for a chance.

"You never cease to amaze me." Randy leaned over and kissed her.

"I don't know about you, but I'm ready to take a shower," Denise said as she put on her knee length, silk black robe she purchased from Macy's just before they left town. She had the same exact one in a smaller size, but it started to hug her a little tighter than usual so she upgraded a size.

"Just let me unpack some of our stuff first," he responded.

"Okay. I'll be getting everything ready," she said while walking into the bathroom. She removed her housecoat and stood in front of the mirror, looking at herself from head to toe. *My full face. Round belly. I'm so surprised he didn't notice. Well, it doesn't matter because, even if he does, I'll just play dumb.*

"Honey, is everything okay?" Randy asked as he entered and overheard Denise mumbling to herself.

"Baby, do you think I'm getting fat?" Denise questioned.

"No babe. Why?" he said, staring at her as if she was insane.

"I don't know. It's just my body looks…"

"You've always been thick. There isn't anything wrong with that. You always look great," he continued and Denise smirked.

"I guess I'm just trippin. That's all," she stated.

"You are cause you look great. Always have." Randy kissed her.

"Thanks honey. You're the best."

After showering, they decided to explore the resort and checked out all of the activities they could take part in while on the island.

The next morning, Randy and Denise arose with the Jamaican sun peeking through the curtains. Denise rolled over and discovered Randy pretending to be sleep.

"Baby, wake up." She decided to play along. He shrugged her off and rolled over in the opposite direction. "Randy!" she continued then he rolled back over, grinning.

"Good morning, sweetie. Breakfast is waiting for us," he said as he jumped out of bed already dressed. She followed him into the nook where plenty of food awaited them.

"Where did you get all this?" Denise's eyes were already full at the sight of eggs, bacon, kiwi, papaya, cantaloupe, and grits while Randy pulled out the chair for her then kissed her again since he couldn't resist.

"Don't worry. I have my ways," he responded before she looked at him and laughed. "I ordered it from the kitchen. The driver brought it up."

"Well, it looks delicious, baby." She spread her napkin on her lap.

Randy fixed Denise some fruit with some grits and was surprised she didn't want any eggs on her plate. She sensed he might be a little suspicious about her not wanting any since she has eaten them every morning as long as they've been married. So, she went into this complete story about the last time she went to McDonalds. She told Randy how she ran late one morning and decided to order an Egg McMuffin but bit into the sandwich and discovered a hair embedded in it. She vowed to never eat eggs again. She managed to convince him she had a horrible experience. But, truthfully, they made her extremely sick. And, if she ate them with the other food, it all would come right back up and out of her mouth.

"This is just what we needed," she said, easily changing the subject while eating.

"You're right. It's just nice not to do anything for a change."

"Baby, I always tell you, you need to slow down and step back sometime. The church will still run smooth because you have enough people in place."

"I know. And honestly, I try, but it's hard. Guess I get that from my father."

"You sure do. And that's exactly why you need to take it easy before you stress yourself to the point of getting sick."

"Are you afraid I'll have a heart attack like my father?"

"To be honest, the thought crossed my mind," she added while Randy grabbed her hands and interlocked them with his.

"Don't worry. I promise from now on, I will start taking care of myself."

"And...?" Denise added.

"And what?"

"And promise me you'll learn how to say no sometimes," she continued. He leaned in and kissed her.

"I promise."

Denise finished breakfast and was truly surprised that she was able to keep it down. Once she finished eating, she got up and dressed so they could go out.

"Isn't this beautiful?" Denise asked as they walked side by side. After a whole day of sightseeing and dinner in front of a live band, a walk along the beach was the perfect way to end the evening.

"It's absolutely wonderful," Randy replied before Denise grabbed one hand as he carried their shoes in the other.

"Exactly what we both needed. It's so easy to get caught up. Being away from you so much is not good. But, that's all going to change. I promise. From now on, you'll come first." Randy spun Denise around in his arms and dropped their shoes onto the vanilla colored sand.

"I love you."

"I love you, too," she said. Then, he looked her directly in her eyes.

"Let's start a family," he continued with excitement in his voice but Denise smiled politely before Randy hugged her.

"You still serious about kids?" Denise asked, hoping he would say he wanted a cat or dog - anything but a child.

"More than you know."

"Don't you think we need some more time? I mean, I don't think I'm ready to be a mother," she explained. He caressed her face.

"You'll be fine. We'll be fine. Besides, I want you to be the mother of my children. And, you know we're not getting any younger. But, we don't have to talk about this right now. We can work everything out when we get home. Hopefully, we can get started real soon," he stated.

Denise kissed Randy when she heard him change the subject. She knew he hoped to start a family soon. But, in actuality, it was already in progress. The baby just belonged to another man. She had to do something before her husband found out. So, she made dealing with it the first issue on her priority list when they returned from vacation.

A week after they got back, Denise sat in the examination room at the doctor's office. She hoped and prayed she wasn't expecting, that the home pregnancy tests were wrong and the illness was some flu-like virus but knew otherwise. She hadn't mentioned anything to Randy because she didn't want to get his hopes up. She knew that, as soon as he heard the news, it would be the happiest day of his life since he seemed so eager to start a family. Denise glanced down at her silver Movado watch and realized she had been waiting for almost an hour. When Randy asked where she was going, she told him over Terri's house however she hadn't told her. Just as she grew extremely impatient, the doctor opened up the large wooden door.

"I'm sorry it took me so long but my office has been so crowded lately. I think it's baby season." The female doctor smiled and Denise tried her best to return one. "You are pregnant, Mrs. Tate."

"I figured I was."

"But, you're further along than you think. According to the tests, you're about three months."

Hold on. Three and a half months. Maybe, I heard her wrong, Denise thought then spoke asked the doctor to repeat herself.

"You're about three weeks shy of four months."

This cannot be happening. I cannot be that far along. Almost four months? Three and a half months ago Randy and I were barely on speaking terms, so I know we didn't have sex, Denise continued to ponder. "Thank you," she said.

"If you have any questions, please feel free to call me," the doctor replied.

As Denise walked across the parking lot, she glanced at her cell phone and realized she missed four calls. One message was from Randy, one was from Terri, and the last two were from Tyrone. She fumbled with her car keys and rain started to fall, which made Denise search even faster so she could hurry home before the storm hit. Because, with the way the sky appeared, you could tell it was around the corner. Denise couldn't stand the rain and hated to be caught anywhere in that condition, while the downfall truly summarized how she felt at that moment as well as signified where her life was headed. She knew it was supposed to be a joyous occasion when a woman finds out she is going to have a baby but, for her, it wasn't. She looked at it as the end of freedom as she knew it.

She listened to the voicemail Terri left, knowing she would ask her to come over so they could talk while the only thing Denise wanted to do was go home and sleep the rest of the day away. But, she called Terri and agreed to stop by later. Now, Tyrone called and left her a message about how he missed and wanted to see her. But, hearing his voice made her sick while being pregnant didn't make the situation any better. So, instead of listening to the second one from him, she deleted it. Then, just as she pushed the button to the garage door, her cell phone rang.

"Hey babe. What are you doing?" Randy asked.

"Just got home from running some errands. Think I'm about to go upstairs and take a nap."

"I was calling to let you know I'm going to be home later than usual. I'm going to be counseling two couples instead of one," he stated.

"Well, do you want me to cook you some dinner?"

"No. I'll just grab us something on my way home."

"I'll see you then," Denise said in between yawning.

"Are you okay? You sound like something's wrong," Randy questioned.

"No. Nothing's wrong, I'm tired, that's all."

"I'll see you in a little while." Randy hung up the phone.

I almost forgot Randy has an up close and personal relationship with the Lord that enables him to sense when something is wrong with me. I'm definitely not ready to tell him, so I have to make sure he doesn't find out yet.

Denise tried to take a nap and get some rest, but she couldn't close her eyes for more than five minutes because her mind was full of thoughts. So, instead, she decided to take a bubble bath, hoping the water, candles, and music would relax her. The fifteen minutes she spent soaking seemed like an hour as she drifted off to sleep. However, someone at the front door interrupted her peaceful nap. Denise stepped out of the tub, slipped on her blue terry cloth robe with matching slippers, and headed downstairs.

She thought it was Terri but, when she looked through the window and saw Tyrone, she wanted to act like she wasn't home. She hoped he would get the hint and leave yet knew he was too persistent and wouldn't until she at least showed her face.

"Hey baby. Long time no see," he spoke as he brushed past her as soon as she opened up the door.

"Randy's not here. He's at the church." She shut the door and closed up her robe even tighter.

"I know. He's counseling. So, I'm actually here to see you."

"What made you think I wanted to see you? Haven't talked to you for the longest time."

"I know. That's why I decided to come see you. We can catch up. So, how was Jamaica?" he asked as he plopped down on the couch. But, Denise never moved. She stood in the foyer with her arms crossed.

"None of your business."

"Why are you so cold, now? You never seem to care about your husband when I'm hitting that spot. You know you still want me." Tyrone got up from the couch and walked over to where she stood.

"It's time for you to leave." Denise looked away toward the door.

"Just admit it." Tyrone moved in closer and began to kiss her on her neck, knowing that made her go absolutely wild every time. And as expected, she dropped her arms to the side and entered into a trance.

"Can't nobody do you like I can. That spot was created just for me because I'm the only one who can find it." Tyrone continued to kiss her neck softly and undo her bathrobe. "I know you've missed me."

Denise tried to open up her mouth and tell him to go to hell but couldn't deny him as the best man she had ever been with sexually. He knew what to do and say. He had skills like someone in the Olympics. And, if sex were a sport, the gold medal would definitely go to him. With all of the good traits he had, there were some bad ones that couldn't necessarily be overlooked. Out of the men she crept around with, he was the most possessive. He felt like, once he had sex with a woman, he marked his territory and she belonged to him forever.

As Tyrone carried Denise to her guest bedroom, she figured she would try to remain as quiet as possible. The less she said, the less trouble she would get in later since he had a habit of taking Denise's words and throwing them back in her face.

"Your body is more beautiful than the last time I saw you." Tyrone laid Denise onto the bed and stared at her nakedness from head to toe. "There's something different about you."

"What do you mean?" Denise asked but was afraid to hear his answer.

"You're getting thicker. Your face is fatter. Hips spreading. And, your stomach is fuller."

Okay genius. Just tell me I look pregnant, she thought. "Is that a problem?"

"Naw baby. Not at all. You look good. You're glowing." Tyrone began to kiss Denise and she smiled. Although she knew he had noticed her weight gain, he didn't figure out she was pregnant and she wanted to keep

190

it that way until her and Randy made the announcement to the church. She was glad he hadn't said the "p" word.

"I'm lying, Tyrone. I do miss you," Denise continued before they proceed to physically connect their bodies.

After Tyrone left, Denise frantically ran around trying to clean up the guest bedroom before Randy came home. The phone rang as she replaced the sheets on the bed so she rushed to the master bedroom to answer it.

"Hey baby." Denise knew it was Randy from looking at the caller I.D.

"You seem out of breath."

"I'm okay. I was coming up the stairs," Denise said.

"I picked up your favorite pasta Alfredo with chicken from Romaine's. I'll be home in ten minutes."

"See ya then."

Denise waited for Randy while thinking about Tyrone's visit. She had just allowed him to come up in her home like he owned the place and didn't even put up a fight. She was mad she actually gave in to Tyrone but her thoughts shifted when Randy opened the door.

"That was thoughtful of you," Denise said as he came in carrying two bags from one of her favorite places to eat.

"I know you love Romaine's so I wanted to do something special for my baby." Randy smiled. Denise lifted her container out of the bag and set it on the kitchen counter.

"I appreciate it." Denise kissed Randy and opened the Styrofoam box. *Oh my God. Another thing I'm not going to be able to eat because the smell is making me nauseous*, she thought as soon as she inhaled her favorite dish. Then, immediately, she let go of Randy's arms and ran to the bathroom. He followed.

"Baby! What's going on?" He prepared and put a damp washcloth over Denise's forehead after watching her vomit in the toilet but she didn't answer.

"I'm going to take you to emergency because you didn't sound like yourself earlier." Denise lifted up her head and looked at Randy.

"No," she said as she reached up and grabbed his hand. *If he takes me to the hospital, he will definitely know. Guess, I need to tell him before he finds out.*

"Why baby?" Randy kneeled down and looked her in the eye.

"I've been sick lately. I made an appointment with the doctor. Basically, I'm pregnant," she stated then Randy's concern instantly turned to happiness.

"Did you just say you were pregnant?" he asked.

"I did." Denise smiled.

"I'm going to be a father?" He grinned from ear to ear.

Randy looks like he just won the lottery. If only he paid attention, he would see my happiness is forced. I'm not ready to be a mother. Not ready to give up my freedom for someone else. And, most of all, I'm not ready to lose this figure. Are you kidding me? And to top it off, Tyrone's the father.

"We're finally going to have a family. This is exciting. I got to call mom and tell her," Randy exclaimed but Denise grabbed his arm as he tried to walk away.

"I'm not sure if I want to tell anyone just yet."

"Why not? This is our first child. I want everyone to know. You have made me the happiest man in the world today." Randy kissed her forehead.

"Since you put it that way. Why don't we invite everyone over for dinner and tell the family at the same time," she said.

"I still want to have something at the church, Denise," Randy explained before he walked down the hallway to his office. She followed him.

Chapter Seventeen

Once Randy learned Denise was pregnant, he refrained from going into the church to work. For four days, he canceled all of his appointments to spend some quality time with Denise at home. She insisted he didn't have to but he told her he wanted to be next to her. He woke up before she did every morning, fixed her breakfast, and ran her a bath then spent most of the day on the Internet looking for things they could buy to put into the baby's nursery. If he wasn't doing that, he flipped through parenting magazines, reading various articles pertaining to having and raising your first child.

"Baby, what do you need me to do for you this morning?" he asked as she awoke.

"At the moment, nothing," Denise said.

"Are you sure? All you have to do is say the word and it's done."

"I'm fine."

"Just want to make sure I'm doing everything I can for you and our child. What do you want to do today?" Randy sat down beside Denise and rubbed her stomach.

"Nothing. I wanna lay around and be lazy. My feet are a little swollen."

"Well, if you don't mind, I'm going to stop by the church and try to catch up on some of my work. But, I'll be right back."

"That's cool, honey! Just call me when you're on your way home," she said.

Denise was glad Randy left instead of being stuck up underneath her all day. She liked the extra attention but couldn't help think about the reality of it all. Not only was her life about to change, she carried another man's child. She never envisioned things turning out this way. She was just trying to pass time and add a little excitement to her existence. She was glad Randy finally knew of the pregnancy but regretted telling him she was two months rather than four. She thought about telling Randy the actual time of her term, but couldn't risk him doing the math and figuring out she conceived when they weren't even sleeping in the same bed. Randy never had a child and probably would not figure out what was really going on, she thought but simply didn't want to take the chance.

Denise managed get up and clean the house a little, including washing some dishes even though her feet started bothering her. Then, just as she took a seat to rest them, the doorbell rang. She answered it and was happy to see her best friend with a smile from ear to ear.

"I just can't believe you're pregnant," Terri said while hugging Denise as she walked in the house.

"So, you got my message."

"Sure did. Almost swerved off the side of the road when I heard it!"

"Why? Were you shocked?"

"Girl, just to hear that come out your mouth. The Denise Tate I knew used to say she wasn't having a baby for nobody. Not even Randy."

"I know what I said. But, truth is, I'm almost four months. I wanted to get an abortion but I'm too far along. Couldn't get an appointment."

"Having your husband's baby is not a bad thing, Denise. It's a part of life."

"Terri, truth is, I'm not pregnant by Randy," Denise revealed as her friend's eyes almost jumped out of her head.

"Are you serious? Well, whose is it them?" Terri asked as Denise looked at her friend but remained silent.

"Oh my God! Don't tell me you pregnant by Tyrone?" Terri asked in disbelief then Denise shook her head to confirm truth.

"Does he know?"

"No! And, I would like to keep it that way."

"So you have no intentions of telling him?"

"I do not," Denise said matter-of-factly.

"Does Randy know you're pregnant?"

"Yeah, he know. And been spending every waking moment with me."

"He thinks it's his?"

"Why would he think otherwise? I'm his wife, Terri. And, this is the beginning of our family."

"Unbelievable! I hope you know how dangerous this can be!"

"I'm know! But, let's be honest what kind of father would Tyrone be for my child? He's already got some major issues. I don't want my child growing up around that fool. So, Randy is the father."

"How are you so sure Tyrone is? Maybe it is Randy's?"

"No, I'm certain," Denise said.

"Aren't you afraid he'll find out one day?"

"I got it all figured out. I'm actually further along than what Randy think. So, when the baby comes, it'll just look like the baby is premature."

"I still don't see how that's going to work."

"Don't worry. It will."

"You can be in denial if you want, but I'll hate to see the day your plan backfires."

"Terri, trust me, it won't. And, that's for sure."

"I hope you're right."

195

"I know. And, I've thought about all that. Trust me, he'll never know otherwise."

Denise understood Terri was only being concerned about her and the situation but truly believed everything was going to be okay as long as she stuck to her story.

"I'm so glad that you and your wife could make it," Randy said as he stepped to the side and allowed the deacon and his wife to enter. Randy was excited since a week had passed and he was unable to share his joy until this moment.

"Anytime the first lady is cooking, I'll be here," the deacon replied.

"Denise, I think my husband likes your cooking more than mine," his wife added.

"Now, baby, you know I think yours is the best in the world. I wouldn't have married you if you couldn't cook." He laughed and she swatted him with her purse.

"Look at the both you. You've been married over twenty years, raised your kids, and still in love," Randy commented then gave them both a hug as they continued to laugh while others began to arrive.

Shortly afterwards, everyone took their places at the dining room table and Randy blessed the food. But, before they started helping themselves, he stood up.

"Prior to us partaking of this feast, I would like to say a few words," he said, then reached over toward his wife who sat next to him. Smiling, she rose from her chair.

"As we stand here together, hand in hand, I thank God that he chose all of us to be connected as a family. I am so grateful for each of you. That's why we invited you over to share this special day with us." He paused. "We're expecting a child." Randy let go of her hand and rubbed her stomach while the family all flooded them with hugs and kisses.

Mama Tate grinned from ear to ear as she embraced Randy then Denise. She told them how she was so excited to finally be a grandmother before Denise's nephews spoke up about how they would finally have a playmate and Michelle expressed her happiness. From there, Mama Tate came and sat down by Denise as the rest of the family ate. She asked when her grandbaby was due to make its debut and Randy responded.

Terri seemed shocked.

"You've made me so happy." Alice gave Denise a hug and a kiss on the cheek. She looked at her mother-in-law and smiled. She never heard those words come out of her mouth and wasn't going to question why, as oppose to accepting it. In Denise's mind, it was about time Mama Tate showed her some respect. "Oh my goodness, you're really starting to show too," she replied while she rubbed Denise's stomach.

"I know. Seem like one day nothing and the next, full-blown."

"Who knows, you might be carrying twins. You look too big for just one. You they run in our family." Mama Tate smiled and Denise forced one in return.

I knew she would say something like this. Why can't she just let me be pregnant? No! Instead of congratulating me like everyone else, minding their business, she had to make a comment... I know she's trying to be nice and all right now, but that's one person I must keep my eye on.

"No, I think I'm just pregnant with one baby. Don't think I could handle two."

"Yeah, they're definitely hard. My sister'll a tell you." Mama Tate smiled.

"I'm sorry. Can you excuse me for one minute?" Denise asked as she saw Jimmy making his way into the kitchen and figured it would be prime time to talk to him. It was also an opportunity to get away from Alice's questions before they got crazy.

"Sure honey. Go ahead," she said.

As Denise walked in the kitchen, she managed to slip in without him noticing. She stood in the corner and watched Jimmy put all of the dirty dishes in the sink. He rolled up his sleeves and started to clean them before turning around to pick up one of the casserole dishes sitting on the counter.

"What I do now?" He looked at her and realized she wasn't smiling.

"You haven't done anything." Denise crossed her arms.

"If you don't want me to wash the dishes, then I won't. I just wanted to help you out since you're pregnant." Jimmy wiped his hands dry with a towel and was on his way out of the kitchen to avoid getting into another argument with Denise.

"Wait a minute. Don't leave," she replied, which caused him to turn around with a confused look on his face.

"I know the last time we talked, I said some things that were out of line and I shouldn't have. But, I just didn't want her going through the same things. When I first saw her back with you, I thought she didn't give you enough time to prove yourself to her. I really felt you hadn't changed."

"Denise, I knew exactly where you were coming from. And, had a right to be mad and say what you said. I did do her and my kids wrong. You're only looking out for her."

"I've been thinking about this ever since. And, I wanted to say. I'm sorry."

"I accept your apology. I really do love my family. I only want to do right by them from now on."

"Good," she said then returned to the dining room.

Denise was glad she patched things up with Jimmy since she'd practically cussed him the last time they were together. She was happy to see he finally decided to get his act together and be the man her sister so desperately needed. Even though Denise would've preferred her sister married someone with a more cash flow, she was satisfied knowing he worked hard and would do his best to provide for them.

Time passed as everyone socialized and, just when Denise decided to go down to the basement and check on her nephews, the doorbell rang so she hurried to the entrance.

"I can't believe you're finally having a baby!" Denise's mom said as she grabbed and hugged her tight.

"Michelle must've already told you." Denise smiled.

"She called me on my cell after you two made the announcement. We were on the highway as soon as we heard," she explained, then looked at her daughter.

"I'm sorry, Denise, I couldn't help myself. I knew they wouldn't be here for a while, so I had to let ma know," Michelle said. "I didn't know she would drive up here."

"You know what? It never fails. You have the hardest time keeping your mouth shut but I guess I'll let it slide this time." Denise smiled as her stepfather kissed her on the cheek.

"I'm so happy for you and Randy," he said.

"Thanks. You and mom didn't think this day was going to come, did you?"

"Denise, I must admit. I've been in the family a long time. I never thought you would be telling us this," her stepfather continued.

"For a while, I thought you were allergic to kids, sis." Michelle laughed and Denise smacked her lips.

"Um. Excuse me. Just because I'm not a baby making machine... bet Jimmy can look at you and you'll get pregnant."

"Whatever. You're just mad because you're about to be fat," Michelle retorted before Randy stepped in between them and acted as if he was a referee. Then, when he got their attention, he decided to throw in his two cents.

"She isn't getting fat, just thick." He put his arms around his wife then his hands on the lower part of her belly.

"Thank you, baby." Denise smiled.

"Besides, I like you with a little extra meat on your bones. It makes me wanna..." Randy stopped when Michelle appeared as it she would throw up, which made the entire room erupt with laughter.

"That's too much information," she spewed.

"No it's not. I don't try and break you and Jimmy up when you two are all in each other's face. Now, do I?"

"That's not the point. The thought of you and my brother-in-law is nasty," Michelle said. Denise held up her hand to silence her before directing everyone's attention to their mother.

"Can I get you anything? We still have a lot of food left in the dining room."

"Please. We haven't eaten since this morning."

"I'll fix you two a plate." Denise started walking in the direction of the dining room while everyone else gathered in the living room where the men put on the Pittsburgh Steelers game. Terri followed Denise into the dining room and helped.

"Denise, your mom and step-dad look good. I haven't seen them in so long. Has she lost more weight?"

"I think she told me she lost like twenty-five pounds. And, had the nerve to tell me she was getting fat so she wanted to lose a little bit more. I told her she was crazy. She was already a size twelve. Now, she's down to an eight."

"Whatever she did, she looks great," Terri stated as she exited the kitchen to carry the plates to the table.

Denise's parent's ate and decided to stay overnight in a hotel so they could spend another day in town. So, after the game ended, everyone left one by one.

"This was great, Denise," Randy said while closing the door as the last guest exited. Then, they stood in front of the picture window and watched them drive off.

"I'm glad you liked it." Denise put her arms around him and inhaled his cologne.

"If we tried to do something like this at the church, it would've been crazy. Everyone seems to be just as excited as we are. My mother was literally bouncing off the walls when we she heard."

"I know. She kept hugging me and kissing me all night. Thanking me for giving her, her first grandchild. It was only fair for the family to know first."

"We made her so happy. She's have been waiting for this since we got married."

"And, get this," Denise continued. "She started rubbing my stomach saying I could be pregnant with twins because it's so big."

Randy laughed as he held onto his wife and pulled her in tight. "It never fails. Every time someone in our family is pregnant, she swears they're having twins. She probably told you that it run in our family and your stomach is too big for you to be a couple of months."

"She sure did."

"Well baby, don't let her scare you. She does that to everybody in our family."

Whew! That was a sigh of relief hearing Randy tell me that. Now, I don't feel like she's singling me out. "I'm not. Just didn't know why she said that," Denise explained.

"That's my mother. You know how she is. And, I don't care what we have or how many we have, just as long as they're healthy."

"Be honest. Do you want a boy or girl?" Denise asked.

"I told you. It doesn't matter to me."

"Baby, you're lying. You know you want a boy." Denise remembered the first time they talked about having children and thought back to how Randy said he would love to have a son. He told her he wanted one that walked, talked, and looked just like him. He even spoke of his son joining him in the ministry and would get a carpenter to build a mini podium to be place right next to his in the pulpit.

"No. I'm not. I'm just praying for our child to have ten fingers and ten toes. That's what's important to me."

"When I have a girl, like I want, I don't want to hear your mouth."

"I won't complain. I'll be the happiest father in the world," he said.

Denise knew Randy was truly happy about becoming a father but, at the same time, recognized that he would be shattered if he ever found out the truth.

So, she promised to never tell him, not under any circumstances.

Chapter Eighteen

Denise grew tired of sitting around the house day after day, not doing anything but resting after first trimester, morning sickness phase passed. She was so happy the throwing up on a regular basis ended. Even though she felt a whole lot better and found herself doing more than she had been, her husband still stopped her from engaging in too many strenuous activities. Randy insisted she get as much relaxation as she could for their child. But to her, that was easy for him to say because he roamed about freely and did as he pleased. And, she grew tired of him relating everything to her being pregnant.

Don't bend over too much. You don't want to hurt the baby. Don't reach over your head. It could hurt the baby. Don't take any baths, Denise, it could hurt the baby. Everything he said had something to do with the baby, she thought as she woke up. *What about me? Has he forgotten that if not for me, this child can't be born?*

Denise picked up the phone and called Terri. She desperately needed to get out of the house and wanted to spend some time at the spa since she couldn't go anywhere else. It had been a few months since her last visit while she usually went every three weeks.

"What are you doing?" Denise asked as soon as Terri picked up.

"Nothing, I have the day off. What you doing? Refolding those baby clothes Randy brought the other day?"

"You got jokes, huh?" Denise teased before asking Terri to join her.

"That sounds good. I'm long overdue for a massage," she replied. Denise got out the bed and headed toward to bathroom to get ready.

While Denise put on one of the only jogging suits that fit over her swollen belly, she got a call from Tyrone. She really wasn't in the mood to answer it but found herself pressing the talk button on her cell phone anyway.

"Why haven't you been answering?"

"Hello to you too."

"Quit the games, Denise."

"I'm not playing games, Tyrone. What are you talking about?"

"You know exactly what I'm talking about. Isn't there something you've forgotten to tell me?" he asked while Denise decided to play aloof.

"I'm sorry. I don't know what you're talking about."

"Really? Well, I was at the church this morning in a meeting with the deacon board, when one started going on and on about you being pregnant. I was completely lost because you haven't told me. So, I figure you forgot."

"I didn't forget to tell you anything."

"Is it true. You're pregnant?"

"Yes, I am," Denise answered in the driest tone possible, but her nonchalant attitude about the whole situation only irritated him more.

"You just weren't going to tell me at all. Just like that?" Tyrone asked.

"I don't have to announce my every move to you and I really don't feel like having this conversation right now. Goodbye." Denise hung up the phone and stuffed it in her purse. She ended the call because she knew he wasn't going to do anything but talk in circles and she wasn't in the mood to deal with his interrogations. Besides, she didn't feel the need to explain anything to him like she was some naive school girl.

Denise walked into the lobby of the spa and saw Terri waiting for her. She looked at her friend, who seemed to be in her own little world text messaging on her Blackberry and so consumed with her phone that she didn't even see Denise walk up to her.

"I haven't been here in months," Denise said as Terri looked up.

"Me either. I really needed this." Terri turned her device off and placed it in her pocket.

"I'm surprised to even see you out today. For the last couple weeks, Randy's had you in baby prison."

"Shut up." Denise laughed as the receptionist took them back to the salon area.

"I'm serious. It's been like a month and a half since you've done anything. If he hasn't let you out of the house, I know you haven't spent time with you know who," Terri commented as her toes entered the foot bath.

"I haven't but I still see him all the time."

"What has he been doing lately?"

"You mean, what hasn't he done? Girl, all in his power to make sure he's around me. Every time I turn around, he's on another committee, serving another board. And, get this. He joined the choir last week."

"I know that made you mad."

"Absolutely furious. But, that's not even the worst part."

"What's going on?" Terri asked and Denise told her about his call earlier that day.

"Isn't he kind of late?"

"Extremely. But, that's just how Tyrone is. He'll wait until the last minute and, when he reacts, he always blows everything up. I know this sound crazy... Even though I can't stand him half the time, there's something that draws me to his insane behind."

"Is it like that?"

"I can't even put my finger on it but he's so seductive. That keeps me going back. But, at the same time, he drives me away with his crazy antics."

"Seems like there's whole love/hate relationship going on."

"I'm not even going to lie, we do. I care about him but can't stand him all in one. Lately, with him being so involved in the church, I haven't been able to put up with him. Then, he called acting like he was mad this morning."

"Do he think you're carrying his child?" Terri asked.

"Why would he think that?" Denise asked and shot her a funny look like.

"Well, I'm sorry to burst your little fantasy bubble but you know you've had sex with Tyrone way more than Randy. So, don't be surprised, Ms. Thing, when he comes to you and thinks it's his," Terri continued.

"Whatever. He better not think this his child because it's not!" Denise tilted her head back and closed her eyes as the nail technician started her pedicure.

Denise didn't want to think about the possibility of Tyrone even considering she was pregnant by him. He was obsessive, territorial, and would assume paternity. However, she would have to make him see he had nothing to do with it. If he couldn't accept it, so what. There would be nothing or no one messing with her plan to raise the baby with Randy.

They finished up their day of total pampering in time for Denise to make it to her doctor's appointment. She drove there straight from the spa, arriving in a matter of minutes. She entered, the nurse escorted her into the room then told her to change into a gown and wait for the doctor, who eventually walked in with a chart in her hand.

"You're pregnancy is progressing just fine, Mrs. Tate," she said.

"I'm glad to hear that," Denise responded.

"Your vital signs are good. All your blood work is normal," she continued as she washed her hands before spreading blue gel over Denise's entire stomach.

"It's always so cold."

"That's what all of my patients say," she replied then placed the monitor on Denise's belly. She saw the image appear on the screen and smiled.

"The last time I was here, you couldn't determine the sex because the baby's legs were crossed. Has it changed positions at all?" Denise lifted her head.

"You are having a girl." The doctor pointed to the screen.

Denise wanted a girl while Randy said he would be satisfied no matter what but she knew he really wanted a boy. In fact, he was so anxious to know the baby sex that he canceled everything he had to do on the days of her doctor's appointments. He wanted his schedule to be clear so he could join her. She told him he didn't have to drop everything. Really, she didn't want him going to the doctor with her so she told him it was still too early to determine the baby's gender.

"Now that you're close to six months, I need to meet with you and your husband next time you come."

"Why? He's so busy."

"We'll need to discuss birthing options," she continued.

"I will do my best to try and get him to come next time," Denise responded.

"I'll see you a month from now," the doctor replied, then removed her gloves, washed her hands again, and exited.

Denise didn't want Randy to come with her until she talked to the doctor about some things. She had to find a way to convince her to go along with her plan and she was willing to do whatever so her secret remained that way.

As Denise drove from the doctor's office, Tyrone called and she rolled her eyes but answered. "What do you want?" she asked.

"Is our baby growing healthy and strong?" he replied and she regretted taking the call.

"Shut up! You know this isn't your baby."

"Whatever. I'm not even calling to start an argument with you. I missed you and trying to see you today. What's up?"

"I can't. Randy and I have other plans."

"Oh. So, you not gone come see me instead."

"Randy is my husband, Tyrone. I can't just cancel my plans like that and you know it." Denise was tired of Tyrone thinking the sun rose and set because of him, fed up with his childish ways. In her mind, he acted like a complete idiot and she was sick of him carrying on like a brat when he didn't get his way.

"Well, I had a feeling you was going to pull a stunt like this today so I got one of my own," he said while Denise could sense him smiling on the other end of the phone.

"What are you talking about?" she asked.

"I hope you're close to home. Because, after I stopped at the church and talked to Randy for a little, I came over to your house. But, you weren't there. So, I decided to leave you a little present."

"What?" Denise spewed.

"And, I called Randy. He is also on his way home. I pray you get there before he does. Otherwise, well, let's just say... you'll have a lot of explaining to do."

Denise ended the call then dropped the phone on her passenger's seat before she put her foot on the gas pedal and pushed it to the floor. She was fifteen minutes from home and hoped she arrived before Randy as she didn't know what Tyrone had up his sleeve. But, whatever it was, it didn't feel right. By the time Denise pulled up to the house and pushed the garage door opener, she realized she beat him home after all.

She picked up her cell phone and got out of her truck. Once she shut the door and pressed the lock button, she saw something taped to the front entrance. As she approached it, her eyes grew wide. On the door, for the entire neighborhood to see, was her black thong with a note addressed to Randy. It read: *THESE BELONG TO YOUR WIFE. SHE LEFT THEM AT MY HOUSE LAST WEEK. OH AND TELL DENISE TO REMEMBER WHAT I SAID. I DON'T HAVE TO REVEAL MYSELF BECAUSE IN TIME YOU WILL KNOW WHO I AM.*

Denise balled up the piece of paper and threw it in the trash then her house phone rang as soon as she walked in.

"Did you make in time," he asked and laughed.

"I hate you!"

"Well, maybe next time I want to see you, you'll find time to come and see me. Or, something else will happen."

"Like what?"

"Try me and you'll see."

Denise walked over to the couch and sat down. She dropped her keys on the floor and began to cry. She felt as if she was in prison since Tyrone turned from her lover to a complete psycho in record time. But, the sad part about it, Denise didn't understand how she allowed it all the happen, how she seduced him to the point where he flocked to her to same way members did to Oakdale. And, she feared what might happen next while being pregnant didn't help the situation. All of Tyrone's antics took a toll on Denise and she wondered how much more could she endure.

Denise heard Randy open the garage door and walk through the kitchen. She grabbed a handful of tissues and tried her best to dry her eyes enough so he wouldn't suspect she was crying. However, as soon as he walked in the living room and looked at her, he dropped everything in his hands.

"Baby, what's wrong? Have you been crying?"

"I'm okay, honey."

"You don't seem okay. Looks like you're upset about something."

"Lately, I've been crying about everything. I think my hormones are out of control."

"Do you want to talk about it? It'll make you feel better." Randy loosened his tie and sat back on the couch. He put Denise's feet in his lap and began to massage them as she rested her head back on the pillow and closed her eyes.

"No, I'm okay. I'm just so glad you're home." She held out her hands and Randy pulled her up close enough so he could kiss her. She wished she could tell him the real reason behind her emotions. Instead, she allowed him to massage her troubles away.

The next morning, Denise woke up to Kirk Franklin's *Imagine Me* playing softly in their bedroom as Randy stood in front of the mirror putting on his cuff links. "Why you let me sleep in, baby. I don't want to make you late for service," she said.

"We won't be late. You seemed peaceful. I didn't want to disturb you." He kissed her on her forehead.

"Thanks honey. I needed that."

Denise went to the walk-in closet and picked out a gray and black maternity suit and held it up to her. It wasn't her favorite but was the only thing that fit. It seemed liked she just went to the mall and bought clothes but there were only three outfits she could actually wear since she grew by the day. She looked at the others, knowing she needed to make another trip to the mall and buy some more things then hurried to get dressed.

Knowing the majority of the church already heard about Denise's pregnancy, Randy still felt like a formal announcement was only proper. They decided to tell the entire congregation about their expecting bundle of joy that day. And, as Randy wrapped up his sermon, he had everyone's attention while there was a full house.

"Before I end service, I want to make a special announcement. Denise, can you join me for this," he said before she got up and made her way to the stage. She smiled because she knew what he was going to say. So, as she walked, she prayed.

When she stepped on stage, she could feel the entire congregation focus on her. If anyone paid close attention to Denise, they would've noticed her stomach was the size of a basketball and her face had gotten pretty fat over the past couple of months. And, since she was even further along than anyone realized, there was no way she could hide it anymore.

"My lovely wife and I want the whole congregation to know we're expecting a child. And, he or she will be here soon. We just wanted to tell you all at once because we love each and every one of you as our own family."

The entire congregation rose to their feet, applauded, and cheered. Randy couldn't even close out service because everyone made their way up to the pulpit to hug and kiss them. Several of the women joked with Denise, revealing they knew she was pregnant but didn't want to say anything until they heard it officially. A couple others disclosed that they suspected the bulge was the result of carrying more than one child.

"You're entirely too big to be only a couple of months," Sister Daphne said. Denise couldn't believe these women had the nerve to even make those comments. But, she knew, when it came down to it, she really did look bigger since six months was a big difference between three and a half.

"I'm so happy you and Pastor Randy are finally having a baby. But, it looks like there's more than one bun in the oven if you ask me. For a minute there, I didn't think you could have children." Sister Daphne continued and gave a funny look that Denise interpreted as she knew what was really going on. Denise opened her mouth in attempt to say something but, out of nowhere, Mama Tate appeared and shut her up.

"You're always in someone's business. Why can't you just be happy for my son and daughter-in-law instead being ignorant?" she exclaimed.

"Well Alice. I wasn't trying to be in their personal business. I was just saying."

"You was saying what? Because, I thought I heard what sounded like a smart remark come out of your mouth," Alice replied and caused Sister Daphne to turn up her nose and walk past Denise. Mama Tate didn't bother to say anything else to Denise. She just winked and continued toward Randy. Denise didn't know why her mother-in-law had come to her rescue but, in that moment, she was thankful.

The entire congregation wished them well. As she hugged person after person, Denise wondered about Tyrone and hoped he had already left. No sooner did she think of him, he made his way to the pulpit toward Randy. She plastered the best smile she could but literally wanted to punch him in his face.

"Congratulations Pastor. I'm so happy for you." He shook hands with Randy then hugged him. As he let go, he made sure he rolled his eyes at Denise. She returned the gesture and crossed her arms. To make matters even worse, he walked right over to her.

"First lady, I'm so happy for you. Give me a hug." He smiled and hugged Denise. But, before he let go, he whispered in her ear, "Don't forget what I said."

Tyrone didn't linger too long around her and Randy. He walked across the congregation hugging everyone in his path like he was the happiest man in the world. Denise couldn't help but to watch him as he paraded across the sanctuary like he owned the church. Just as he was about to walk out, he got her attention and winked at her but she could feel herself getting nauseous.

Chapter Nineteen

"Is the doctor in her office?" Denise asked the receptionist as she entered the suite.

"Yes, she is," she responded.

"Can you let her know I'm here?"

"She's finishing up with another client but I'll definitely tell her."

The receptionist turned around to her computer screen and began typing. Denise walked over and sat down in one of the plush lounge chairs. She knew her doctor would be surprised because her next appointment wasn't for another two weeks. However, Denise had to talk to her soon as possible. Since she first saw the doctor and confirmed her condition, she avoided bringing Randy. She claimed he was to busy with the church and could never make the appointments. But, as time grew closer and closer to her due date, she knew couldn't continue to avoid it. So, she had to speak with her doctor and straighten some things out before hand.

"You can go back now. She's ready." The receptionist opened up the door and Denise walked through it and down the hall. When she reached it, she smoothed a piece of hair and entered.

"Hello, Denise. What brings you in? Is everything okay? You're appointment isn't for another two weeks, right?" The doctor opened her book and flipped through pages.

"Yeah, but I wanted to talk to you before my next appointment."

"Are you nervous about giving birth? Concerned about something?" She motioned for Denise to sit down.

"Well... sorta. And, I want to talk to you about it."

"What is it?"

"Well. I've been telling you for months that my husband hasn't been able to make it because he's been busy down at the church. But, actually, I told him he didn't have to come," she explained

"Why Denise?" The doctor interrupted with a concerned look on her face.

"Because, I can't have him figure out the truth about my pregnancy."

"What truth? He knows, right? Anyone can see that."

"He knows," Denise continued with confidence. "He just doesn't know how pregnant I am. He thinks I'm only three months," she continued.

"Okay... Why does he think that?"

"I mean. I wasn't sure if I was pregnant in the beginning. After a while, once I found out I was so far along... and..." Denise replied as she tried to convey the reason without revealing too much information. *Come on. I really need to get myself together. I know she can tell something is up. I sound like a complete idiot right now. I really have to stop fumbling over my words.*

"Hold on, Denise. You're not really making any sense. What's the real reason why you neglected to tell your husband?"

"I, I didn't tell him the truth. Because, if I did, I figured he'd put two and two together and discover we weren't even speaking to each other when this child was conceived."

"Have you at least told the father?"

214

"No. I feel it would be best if he didn't know at all."

"And, you're not at all concerned about your husband learning the truth? He hasn't been suspicious at all?"

"This is his first child. So, he really doesn't have a clue when it comes to this stuff. And, I don't plan on telling the father because, as far as I'm concerned, he's not. My husband is. That's why I need to talk to you. I've come up with something I know will work. But, I will need your cooperation to see it carried out."

"What are you talking about?"

"I was thinking that since you are my primary care physician as well as the one who's responsible for delivering my baby, you could help me keep this between us."

"Keep what?" the doctor asked, as she raised both of her eyebrows.

"Like the actual length of my term."

"Don't you think he's going to get suspicious when you deliver the baby two months early?"

"He might, but we can just make it seem like the baby's premature."

"I don't think I can do this. I could get in a lot of trouble," she responded, but it wasn't what Denise wanted to hear. She hoped to come in, present her situation, and the doctor agreed with no if, ands, or buts about it. At the same time, Denise expected she might hesitate so she withdrew ten thousand dollars from the bank earlier that day just in case she needed to drop a little bit of cash in the doctor's lap.

"I understand you have a lot of questions. But, I want you to know where I'm coming from." Denise opened her purse and pulled out the envelope stuffed with money, then placed it on the desk before pushing it toward her. The doctor opened it up.

"What's this for?" she asked.

"A little something for you. So that we're on the same page."

The doctor flipped through the stacks of crisp bills, still bound together. "Denise, I don't know about this," she continued with pessimism. Denise smiled as she saw her look at it again then slip it in her desk drawer.

With the doctor on her side, Denise let out a sigh of relief. She felt like some weight had been lifted off her shoulders and was glad she dealt with the situation as she gave thanks then stood up and walked out of the door.

Denise stopped at Terri's house before going home. And, as soon as she saw her standing in the doorway, she started laughing.

"What's so funny?" Denise said, standing on the porch and trying to cross her arms but her stomach prevented her from doing so.

"The last time I saw you, you're stomach wasn't that big. It's like you're about to explode."

"Feels like it." Denise rubbed it and walked inside.

"I'm surprised you can even drive."

"Actually, I haven't even left the house in a week. It's like, the closer and closer I get to my due date, the more uncomfortable I become. I had a meeting with the doctor today."

"Did you find out what you're having yet?"

"Oh, I didn't tell you already?"

"No Miss Thing. What are you having?"

"A girl."

"She'll probably act just like you. Have you and Randy picked any names out yet?"

"We're going back and forth between a couple but haven't decided."

"I'll help you. Name her Terri and everything will be alright." She laughed and Denise threw a pillow in her direction but missed.

"I swear. If I wasn't so fat I would come over there and slap you in your head."

"Has anything changed with Tyrone?" Terri changed the subject.

"No. He's still crazy. Calling me non-stop. Leaving all kind of stupid voicemails and stopping over whenever he pleases." Denise rolled her eyes.

"So, he still won't leave you alone?"

"Somehow, he's convinced himself that he's the father of my baby," Denise said, before she went on to explain the panty situation.

"Please tell me Randy didn't see that?" Terri responded and Denise described the outcome. "You really don't plan on telling him he's the father, huh?"

"I already told you. I haven't changed my mind."

"I can see why he thinks that though."

"And why is that?" Denise asked.

"I can't even count the nights you've called and had me cover for you."

"I don't care. That don't mean anything."

"You know how he is. He was going to come to that conclusion regardless."

"As far as I'm concerned, he needs to just leave me alone and let me and my husband raise our child together."

Terri laughed. "You know that's not going to happen. I don't know what you did to Tyrone but that man is hooked on you like a holy spirit."

"I know. He can't get enough of what I got." Denise smiled.

"You can make jokes all you want but you better be careful because, if he pulled that thong stunt, who knows what he'll do next. Didn't I tell you that before?"

Denise tried to make light of the situation because she was around Terri but knew things with Tyrone were very serious. Just thinking about him had her stressed out, unable to sleep most nights and, honestly, afraid.

"Now, I know he's crazy. But, he's not that crazy. If he knew what was good for him, he would leave me alone."

"Denise, you know Tyrone does whatever he wants. He isn't scared of you, your husband, or anyone else. I don't even think he's scared of God."

"Like I said, he better not try something else. Or, the next time, you'll read about his life in the obituary section of *The Vindicator*."

"Okay, Miss Gangsta! Whatever you say. Don't even worry about it. All you need to be concerned with is having a healthy baby," Terri replied.

"You're right. I'm not worried. Just as long as my child is blessed, that's all that matter."

When Denise left Terri's house, she suddenly had an urge to eat some barbecue so she made the necessary drive downtown to Charlie Staples BBQ. She was only going to order some saucy chicken and fries for her and Randy. But, when she finally got to the front of the line, her cravings demanded she also order a half slab of ribs, coleslaw, a cup of chili, and a whole sweet potato pie. She was extremely hungry and felt like she would consume all of the things she ordered. The waitress looked at her like she was crazy when she opened up her mouth to place it but she didn't care.

As she sat down to wait for her food, she was surprised to see Tyrone walk through the door. Out of all the people she could've run into, she had to encounter him. As he approached her, she mumbled a few expletives underneath her breath and prayed she wasn't loud enough for God to hear her. She hoped Tyrone would see her and keep moving but knew that, with him, it was impossible.

"Long time no see." Tyrone smiled and found a seat next to her in the booth where she sat.

"Hi Tyrone," Denise said through clenched teeth.

"What's wrong with you? You act like you're not happy to see me."

"Whatever, what are you doing here?"

"The same exact thing you're doing. Ordering food."

"I thought you told me you hated barbeque."

"Naw. I never said that."

"Yes. You did."

"I just had a taste for C. Staples today," he explained. Denise looked at Tyrone and could tell he was lying by the expression on his face.

"Alright, I just missed you. That's all."

"What are you saying? You followed me here?"

"Hmmm. Follow is such a strong word. I didn't follow you, if you're trying to imply I'm a stalker. I just rode in my car behind yours all day to make sure you got to where you needed to go safely. That's all. That is my child you're carrying and I have to make sure I protect mine."

"Are you really serious?"

"Dead serious. What's wrong with you?" Tyrone asked with confusion.

"What's wrong with me? You won't leave me alone. That's what's wrong with me. It's bad enough I constantly see you in church and all. Now, you're following me too. Just leave me alone. What we had is over! So, if you'll excuse me." Denise attempted to get up from the booth and leave but he grabbed her wrist firmly, which caused her to sit back down. Denise hoped he wasn't about to make a scene in the crowded restaurant as she prayed he would act like he had some sense and just let her leave. For a minute, he looked around at people to make sure no one saw him then gripped her wrist even tighter.

"Listen to me. There is no way I will ever leave you alone. So, you can forget about that. Second, since you're having my baby, we're going to always be apart of each other's lives. That is my seed you're carrying."

"You're ridiculous."

"Call it whatever. You still haven't denied I'm that baby's father."

"You are not my baby's father. Why can't you get that through your thick skull?"

Tyrone tightened his grip even more. "Now, understand this. You better act like you got sense and come clean with everything before I do it."

"You wouldn't."

"Believe me. If you don't make this right, you're gonna be sorry you ever knew me." Tyrone got up from his seat and stormed out. She watched him speed out of the parking lot and didn't know what to do next. She was really at a loss for words and didn't even have an appetite. She paid for the food she ordered and told the waitress to bless somebody else with it and went home to relax for the evening.

Randy exited the bathroom the next morning and discovered Denise sitting on the side of the bed rubbing her stomach.

"Good morning, baby. How you feeling?" he asked, but it took her a minute to respond because she was out of breath and it seemed like in effort to answer him.

"I'm not the best. But, I'm okay," Denise said then released a long sigh.

"Are you in pain?" he asked as he walked over and sat beside her.

"I've been in a little, lately. I can feel kicking more and more. This is where it's at," Denise placed Randy's hands on the lower part of her abdomen for him to feel it.

"Should I call the doctor? I don't know a lot about pregnancy. But, I do know you shouldn't be in pain like this." Randy reached for her cell phone on the nightstand. Before he reached it, she grabbed the device.

"No, you don't have to call her. I already did, yesterday. She said it's just from the baby moving around and told me to call back if it gets any worse," Denise lied. She hadn't talked to her since the last time in her office.

"Are you sure? You don't look good."

"Randy, I'll be fine. I just need to lay down and take it easy today. That's all."

"Well, I was going down to city hall and have a meeting with some of the councilmen but I'm going to stay here with you instead." Randy helped Denise get back into bed and pulled the covers up over her entire body.

"Honey, I told you I'll be fine. Go! Have your meeting. Don't cancel your plans."

"You know all I have to do is make one phone call and my meeting is over. Besides, you know you and the baby is more important to me."

"If I need you then I will call." She gave Randy a quick peck.

"Denise, I'm not playing with you. The very minute you need me… I'm home just like that!"

"I promise."

"I'm going to call you every hour," Randy said as he exited the room.

After he left for his meeting, Denise tried to get at ease in bed. But, every time she changed positions, she found herself even more uncomfortable and unable to breathe so she decided to get up and go downstairs to the living room. Just as she managed to sit down on the couch and sink into the leather cushions, she heard someone stick a key into her front door and unlock it.

"Who is it?" Denise asked as she tried to get back up but her belly knocked her right back down.

"It's your sister." Michelle walked into the living room and dropped the bags she carried to the floor.

"Oh, what brings you my way?" Denise put a pillow behind her back and pressed up against it.

"To check on you. See how you were doing?" Michelle took off her coat and hung it over the back of a chair.

221

"I'm miserable. Feels like it's getting heavier everyday. I'm having lower back pain out of this world. And, over the past two days, it feels like I've been having contractions."

"Welcome to the wonderful world of motherhood." Michelle laughed and Denise rolled her eyes.

"You're not helping me at all here."

"I'm sorry, Denise."

"And not only have I been in pain for the past couple of days, Randy has been watching me like a hawk. I practically begged him to go to his meetings today."

"You know this is ya'll first child. He's excited. He wouldn't have it any other way."

"He sent you over here, didn't he?" Denise giggled.

"He did."

"It never fails," Denise stated as Michelle lifted her feet up and propped them up on the coffee table with pillows.

"You should be elevating them so they don't swell," she instructed.

"I know. But, with the baby moving around so much and these contractions, I haven't been able to rest at all."

"It's too early for that. You're probably experiencing Braxton-Hicks."

"You're right. Probably false, huh." Denise put both of her hands on her stomach.

"What you need to sit down and relax. Quit trying to do everything," Michelle said before she went on to spent an hour cooking, cleaning, and putting laundry away just so Denise wouldn't be tempted and try to do it all herself. Normally, Denise would've tried to get up and help at some point, but had to admit, with the way she felt lately, it was nice to have someone complete that work for a change.

"Thanks for coming over," she said as she wrapped up the chores.

"No problem. You did it for me when I was pregnant, both times. I'm just so excited because I going to be an aunt."

"At least you're excited. I'm so nervous."

"Why?"

"I don't know nothing about being a mother. What if I mess up or something?"

"Don't worry about. You're going to be a great. You and Randy both," Michelle reassured but Denise started to cry so they hugged.

"I'm so scared," she continued. For a minute, Denise contemplated telling her sister the truth or keeping her secret. She hated the fact she had to keep the truth from her, but Michelle didn't even know she had an affair. Denise pulled tissues from the Kleenex box and dried up her tears and all the thoughts of her coming clean. She spent too much time and money devising her plan so it was too late in the game.

"Where are my nephews at?" she asked.

"Jimmy took them to the swimming pool down the street from the house. They begged me to tag along, but I made 'em go with him."

"You could've brought them with you. I haven't seen them in a while."

"They didn't need to be over here, running all over the place, getting on your nerves. Besides, every time they hear me say your name, they think you've already had the baby." Michelle shook her head and giggled.

"Those are my crazy little boys."

"You got it right. Definitely crazy."

Before Michelle left, she made sure she finished the things Denise would've tried to do so she had no choice but to lay down and get some rest. Denise even admitted to being more relaxed to herself since her sister's visit.

She managed to lift her legs up onto the couch, turned the CD player on, and drifted off to sleep.

Chapter Twenty

Denise opened her eyes, from her nap, and saw Tyrone standing over her.

"I've missed you so much," he said.

"How did you get in my house?" She jumped up from the couch.

"Let's just say, you need to make sure all of your doors are locked before you decide to go to sleep," he replied. Denise thought Tyrone was lying, until she remembered her sister probably forgot when she left.

"I would appreciate it if you leave. This has gotten ridiculous, Tyrone!"

"I was sent over here to check on you," he calmly stated.

"What are you talking about?" Denise said back down on the couch.

"Randy. He sent me over to see if you needed anything."

"My husband wouldn't do that," she exclaimed but Tyrone laughed.

"Well, after the meeting we had downtown, he mentioned wanting to come home and check on you but only had twenty minutes until his next one. Since he was so worried about you, I told him I would do it for him."

"How thoughtful of you," Denise said in a sarcastic tone.

"I had to, especially since you don't come to see me or return my calls anymore."

"Have you ever stopped to think that maybe I don't want to."

"What you trying to say, Denise?"

"I'm tired of going back and forth with you. The constant phone calls, all these pop up visits. It's too much for me. I think we would be better off if we went our separate ways."

"What?"

"I don't think continuing to see you is a good idea. It's time to move on and put what we had behind us," she attempted to explain but he fall to grasp understanding.

"Just like that, huh? You can't just end what we have in one sentence, just walk away so easily. You know good and well that's my seed."

"This isn't..."

"Come on, Denise. Don't try to play me like I'm stupid. I know it's mine. I wasn't born yesterday."

"I don't even care if I am. You've got a lot of nerve coming up in my house like this. You got to go." Denise jumped up again, extended her arm, and pointed to the door.

"What did you just say?"

"Get out!" Denise asked as Tyrone rose to his feet as well.

"No. Before that?"

"What are you talking about?"

"I knew the baby's mine. You trying to convince yourself otherwise."

"You're crazy"

"I'm crazy? You're the one that's crazy. I expected you to do the right thing before I had to make you." Tyrone pulled Denise's shirt by the collar and pulled her in close to him. "Now, you listen and listen good. I've been trying to sit back and not say nothing about our relationship but it's getting harder and harder."

"I can't breathe," Denise interrupted and gasped. "Tyrone, let me go."

"I will not stop until we're together. And, if you value your life, the life of this unborn child, you'll do things my way."

Denise managed to free herself from his grip and fell, screaming out in pain, so Tyrone panicked. When he knelt down beside her, he noticed a puddle of water on the floor.

"I think I'm in labor!"

Denise was able to stand and wobble into the bathroom to change her pants. Luckily, she had her overnight bag already packed in the coat closet. After she grabbed it, Tyrone helped her into his car.

"Slow down, fool. I'm having a baby, not dying," Denise managed to say in between breaths but he ignored her and kept on driving.

"If you don't slow down, I swear I'll get out and walk."

"That won't be necessary. Just chill. I'm trying to get you there as fast as possible," Tyrone continued as Denise released a loud scream.

"Sounds to me like I need to speed up."

"Whatever! Did you call my husband?"

"He's on his way."

By the time Tyrone pulled up to the emergency entrance at St. Elizabeth Hospital, Denise's whole family had arrived. He wheeled her into the entrance and Randy was the first to greet them at the door.

"Baby! Are you okay?" He kneeled down and kissed her forehead. She grabbed onto his hand and squeezed it.

"I'm fine. Just, these contractions got worse and worse."

"Well, they already have your suite ready," Randy said before the tall thin nurse started to wheel Denise toward the elevator.

After Denise came out of surgery and was stabilized, the nurses allowed the family to see her.

"Hey everybody," she said as they came in and stood around the bed.

"How are you feeling?" Michelle rubbed her face.

"Like I was run over by a semi." Denise tried to laugh, but stopped and held her stomach because she was in pain. "That hurts." She managed to smile.

"I'm just glad you and the baby's okay." Terri came up to Denise and kissed her on her forehead.

"What's her name?" Denise's nephew asked.

"Kaylah Jenae Tate," Denise answered. "And, she's absolutely beautiful. I cannot wait for you to see her."

"Where is my grandbaby? I want see her," Mama Tate questioned as she sat down in one of the chairs next to Denise's bed.

"The nurses said, as soon as they're finished with her, they will bring her in so she can make her debut."

"Well, they better hurry up because I'm ready to see my niece," Jimmy said as Michelle shook her head.

"Calm down, crazy man. You know how long it takes for them to check the baby out. So, quit acting up or else," Michelle stated.

"Or else what?" Jimmy smiled.

"Keep questioning me and you'll find out." Michelle bit her bottom lip.

"Listen, I just had a baby. And now, you two are going to make me throw up." Denise acted as if she was getting sick to her stomach.

"Be quiet, sis. We can't help it if we're in love," Michelle explained while Jimmy hugged her from behind and kissed her cheek.

"You better be careful before she pops up pregnant," Denise replied just as the doctor and nurse walked into the room.

"Where's the baby? I want to see my granddaughter," Mama Tate responded.

"In the nursery. We have her under the radiant warmer because her temperature keeps dropping."

"Is that normal?" Denise inquired.

"Some newborns have a little trouble maintaining their warmth, but that problem usually resolves itself in a couple of days."

"Thank God!" Randy let out a sigh of relief.

"But, we have another issue we need to take care of right. We took a sample of Kaylah's blood and her cell count is very low. That may be what's contributing to the low pressure."

"What can be done for that?" Denise asked.

"We'll need to give her a transfusion," the doctor answered.

"Well, that's fine with us. Whatever you need to do is okay," Denise replied.

"We think that it would be best if she received the blood from a parent since she's so young."

"That's fine. I'll do it." Denise answered before Randy could even speak.

"You lost so much during delivery. You're not a candidate." The doctor said while looking Denise in the face as she began to panic.

Her worst nightmare was unfolding right before her eyes.

"I'll donate," Randy said then attempted to follow the nurse out the room.

"Doctor, isn't it dangerous to give a newborn a transfusion?" Denise interjected, which caused Randy to stop dead in his tracks.

"If Kaylah doesn't receive a transfusion, she could get very sick and might not make it," the doctor explained.

"I don't think she should receive blood," Denise insisted. She sat up and on the edge of the bed then started to cry.

"Baby, don't worry. I'll donate mine and Kaylah will be fine." Randy reached out to hold her hand.

"No!" Denise screamed and pulled Randy's arm when he tried to move.

"Denise, do you realize this is emergency? What's wrong with you?" Michelle asked.

"Randy! You can't give your blood," Denise said with tears streaming down her face. She had tried to keep herself composed for as long as she could but lost all control.

"What are you talking about? You can't. I have to," he said with a confused look on his face.

The moment of truth arrived so Denise lifted up to look Randy in the eyes. For too long she lied but, at that point, was forced to come clean in order to save her daughter's life.

"Randy, you can't. You can't give her blood because... Because you're not the father," Denise confessed with tear filled eyes then covered her face with her hands.

Everyone in the room, including Mama Tate, was speechless. It was so quiet that if a pin dropped to the floor, its sound would be too loud.

"I'm not Kaylah's father? I'm not Kaylah's father! What are you saying?"

"Baby, I am so sorry," she said in between sobs. "I never meant for you to find out like this."

"How was I supposed to find out, Denise! When was you going to tell me!" Randy paced back and forth across the room.

"I am really sorry! What else do you want me to say? I can't take it back."

"If I'm not the father then who is," Randy asked Denise, which caused her to start crying again.

"Who is he, Denise," he exclaimed. She looked up at him and took a deep breath.

"Tyrone," she stated.

"I knew it! I knew you were doing wrong! I wasn't able to put my finger on it but the proof is in the pudding now!" Mama Tate shouted, shaking her head.

Denise could barely see around the room because her eyes were complete full with tears. She didn't even care about her mother-in-law saying nasty things in the background. Instead, she focused on Randy and how he was reacting. She attempted to reach out and grab for him but he pulled away.

"Don't touch me! How could you do something like this?" he asked as tears rolled down his cheeks.

"I'm so sorry. I never meant to hurt you like this. I'm sorry," Denise replied.

"How long have you and Tyrone been seeing each other?"

"We're not still seeing each other."

"I didn't ask you if you were still seeing him. I asked you how long have you been sleeping around with him behind my back?" he shouted while the family listened and the staff exited the room, closing the door to allow some privacy.

"A year and a half."

"So, you knew him before he joined the church?"

"I never knew he was going to join the church. I'm really sorry about this, Randy. Don't you believe me?" Denise pleaded. Randy held up his hand and stopped her.

"You can save your little apology. It's sad because I almost believed you. I'm gone," Randy replied and stormed out of the hospital room.

Denise lost all sense of composure as she watched him leave and Jimmy follow. She was at a loss for words, didn't know what to say. Her sister, Michelle, joined her at her bedside and was silent. Instead, she wrapped her arms around her and silently prayed.

Michelle looked up and saw Tyrone entering. "I don't think you should be coming in here right now, after all that has happened."

"Why not, I'm the father. I have a right to be in here." He flashed the smile that used to make Denise melt but it then made her sick.

"I just don't think it's a good idea," Michelle replied as she walked up to him and got in his face. However, a nurse interrupted the alteration.

"I'm sorry, but we need to get in touch with the biological father as soon as possible. Can someone contact him?"

"I'm the father." Tyrone smiled from ear to ear like he had just won a contest on the radio or something.

"If you'll follow me, we'll need to take your blood so we can start this whole process." The nurse grabbed Denise's chart off the edge of the bed and Tyrone followed suite right behind her.

"I'll be right back. I have to go and give blood to my daughter."

Chapter Twenty-One

With all of the events taking place over the course of a day, Denise felt like she was in the middle of a bad dream. She tried to sleep after her room cleared, hoping things would be better when she woke up. But, instead of getting a nice, uninterrupted nap, she tossed and turned while replaying those events in her mind.

"I didn't know you were still here," Denise said when she rolled over and saw Terri sitting in the chair next to her.

"You know I'm not leaving you alone after what happened."

"I still can't believe it."

"It almost seems unreal."

"I know you want to say, I told you so. Alice sure didn't hesitate. She called me so many names before she left."

"Don't even worry about her. You know how she is when it comes to her son."

"Where is he, Terri?"

"I don't know. He left a while ago and no one's heard from him. He won't answer any of his phones."

"How's Kaylah?"

"She's doing great. The doctor was just in here a little while ago saying all her vital signs are returning to normal."

"I'm glad," Denise said, relieved.

"Ever since the doctor gave her that transfusion, she's made a complete turnaround."

"Please. Tell me Tyrone left already," Denise asked. She did not want to see him at all if she could avoid it. That man knew how to get underneath her skin and on her nerves in a way nobody else mastered.

"I haven't seen him since he donated his blood."

"Well good. I hoped he vanishes into midair. I can't stand him," she continued. Terri began to laugh and Denise didn't find it funny one bit.

"Does it look like I'm laughing? I mean, out of all the people in the world, why does he have to be the father of my baby?"

"That's a question I definitely don't have the answer to."

"You know what? I am so hungry. I haven't eaten all day and I really don't want hospital food."

"Why don't I go out and grab us something," Terri replied.

"That would be nice…"

"Will you be okay until I get back?"

"I'll be fine." As Denise waited for Terri to return, she picked up her cell phone and hit the number three to dial Randy.

"Please, pick up," she kept repeating to herself, hoping he would so she could feel some relief. And, with each ring she hoped and prayed, but he didn't answer.

"Hey baby. It's me. When you get this message, please call me back. We need to talk. I love you." Denise pressed the end button then dialed the house as well as his personal phone number three more times before giving up. She knew Randy ignored her on purpose because his phone was usually attached to his hip. So, she decided to give him some space and sort through everything. And, when ready, he would come back around.

While Denise waited for Terri to return, she drifted off to sleep only to wake up to the sound of a deep voice.

"Hey beautiful," Tyrone whispered into her ear.

"What are you doing here?" Denise rolled over and sat up in the bed.

"Just coming over to check on my girls," he smiled.

"Why can't you just leave me alone? I don't want to be bothered?"

"Come on, Denise. You can't treat the father of your child like that."

"Huh, watch me." She rolled her eyes.

"That's not the way to be. We have a baby together now."

"Do you think I care!"

"Well, I do. That's why I'm here."

"Oh please, Tyrone."

"I'm serious. Ever since I first met you, I knew it was something about you. And, even when you said you were pregnant, I just knew I was the father. Something in me is drawn to you. Now, I feel like we have a chance."

"A chance for what?"

"For us to be together. To raise our daughter. Be a real family."

"You can't be serious. You knew what you were getting into when we first met."

"But, that didn't stop you from having sex with me three to four times a week. You wasn't worried about your marriage then."

"Look! What we had was fun while it lasted. But, if you think I'm going to leave my husband for you, you're wrong. I'm the first lady, always have and always will be. I don't know what you thought."

"If that's how you want it, then fine. But, mark my words. You're going to regret everything you just said." Tyrone got up and stormed out.

Denise didn't know how to take his final statement, not comprehending if it was an actual threat or him trying to play with her mind. But, whatever it meant, she prayed he was pissed off enough to leave her alone. She was tired of having to play the role of an elementary teacher and spell it out to him.

A couple days passed and Denise still hadn't heard anything from Randy. She called him so many times and left messages then began to wonder if she turned into a stalker. She worried about his whereabouts and what he thought. It was unlike him to completely isolate himself from her, even when he was mad. She knew he was dealing with a lot, but never thought he would shut her out completely. Since she hadn't talked to him, she called Michelle to pick her and the baby up from the hospital. And, after Denise took a shower and got dressed, she packed all of the cards, gift baskets, and clothes from church members. Then, suddenly, there was a knock at the door and Denise hollered for whomever to enter. With her back turned, assuming it was her sister, she spoke.

"Thanks for coming. I tried to get in touch with Randy and he hasn't called back so…"

"It's not Michelle," he said. Denise was so shocked to hear Randy's voice. She thought she imagined it.

"I didn't expect you to be here," she said.

"I know. When I called your sister, she told me she was going to get you. So, I told her I would come instead."

"That was nice of you," she stated as she continued to gather her belongings.

Once they left the hospital, Randy didn't say a word to Denise while the silence made her nervous because he always had something to say. By the time they pulled up in the driveway of their home, Denise decided she didn't care what she had to do. She was willing to carry out whatever to make sure Randy wouldn't leave her. She had become too accustomed to living comfortably and wasn't about to let it all be taken away. She walked past Randy into the living room where Kaylah rested in her car seat, picked her up, and sat on the couch. And, when the baby cried, Denise held her against her chest.

"What's wrong with mommy's girl?" Denise looked down at Kaylah. She began to sniff and realized her diaper needed to be changed.

"Let me clean the baby," she said as she went through the process then looked at the newborn as she lay there content. Her little hazel eyes scanned the room to take in her new surroundings. Kaylah was too young to have a care in the world and Denise hoped it would stay that way. She wished Randy was her father instead of Tyrone more than anything, as she never expected to be tied to him forever. But, their child bound them together whether she liked it or not.

"Denise, I need to talk to you," Randy said out of the clear blue, as he entered the living room and sat across from her. She put Kaylah back in the seat and turned the flat screen plasma T.V. off.

"I'm listening." Denise placed the remote on the coffee table.

"These past days have been really hard for me. I've been going through so many emotions, I haven't really talked to anyone except Jimmy," he explained.

"Honestly," he continued, "when I found out Kaylah wasn't mine, I could've put my hands around your neck and strangled you. That's how mad I was. But, that's not even in my character to act like that. I just can't believe you would do something like this to me." Randy paused to collect his thoughts and Denise took it as her cue to speak.

"I've been doing some thinking too. I'm so sorry…"

"Denise, I told you in the beginning of this conversation, I need to talk to you! This is some of the stuff I want to get off my chest," Randy cut her off. Not wanting to interrupt him anymore, she held her hand out and motioned for him to continue. She was surprised to see this new side of him.

"I've been trying to figure what I did that would make you want to step out on me, been beating myself up over this. Then, I concluded this isn't my fault," he continued. "I was ready to just walk away from you. From our marriage. But, after talking with Jimmy, he helped me to see things in a different light. I'm glad he did because I was to ready to give up on you, but I believe in marriage. What you did has hurt me bad."

"And I take responsibility for that," Denise replied, but Randy shot her a look suggesting she needed to keep her mouth shut while she did.

"By all means, I have a right to divorce you today and move on with my life. There are plenty of women ready and willing to take your spot and not even think twice about you. But, for some reason, I can't push myself to make that type of move because I love you. And, love doesn't give up. It's everlasting. The natural part of me wants to be done with you yet the spiritual side isn't ready. I'm not going to ask why you did it. Don't even want to know. But, I am willing to work this out. What do you think?"

"I mean, I feel the same way. I'm just so sorry I even put you in this situation. I never meant to hurt you." Denise looked up at him and started to cry. She didn't even think she was capable of showing emotion on the spot but was desperate. She wanted him to believe she was sorry for her ways and, if she had to shed some tears to increase her credibility, then that was what she would do.

"I understand. But the fact of the matter is, it still happened. So, the first step is we've established we want to make our marriage work. Now, if you're really willing to do this then it'll have to be my way."

"Okay Randy…" Denise answered.

"I had a feeling you were going to say that. So, just to let you know, Tyrone will be coming over here shortly for our next step."

"And, what will that be?"

"Well, I need to talk to him. So, I invited him to come over. He was kind of hesitant at first but finally agreed."

"Honey, I really don't want to see him right now. He's been up at the hospital every day harassing me. He won't leave me alone."

"I figured he would. That's why I've come up with a little plan I think will work. You don't you worry about him at all because I got this." Randy smiled at Denise and she wondered what in the world was going through his mind and prayed whatever he plotted would put Tyrone in his place.

Denise was on pins and needles waiting for Tyrone to arrive. She didn't necessarily want to see him but was more interested in hearing what her husband had to say. And, when the doorbell rang, Randy was already at it to meet him.

"Thank you for coming," he said while ushering Tyrone in. He walked past Randy then saw Denise sitting at the dining table.

"Hello, Denise," Tyrone said. She could tell, by the way he spoke, he tried to flirt with her but she ignored him. Then, Randy entered and sat next to Denise, who still had no clue as to what was up his sleeve. She knew that, whatever he had planned, it had to be clever because he didn't even seem to be bothered by Tyrone's presence.

"Let me get straight to the point. Not beat around the bush." Randy folded his hands on the table and looked

Tyrone eye to eye. Denise glanced over at him. Sweat beads began to form on his forehead and the mere sight of it caused her to chuckle.

"Never in a million years would I have thought I'd be going through a situation like this. But, nonetheless, here I am. Here we are. And, I didn't have any control over what happened between you two in the past, but definitely can determine the future." As Randy spoke, he reached for Denise's hand and held it.

"My wife and I have mutually decided to work on our marriage and raise our daughter together."

"So, where do I fit in this picture, Randy?" Tyrone's nostrils flared.

"Nowhere."

"What are you saying?"

"As easy as you seemed to appear in our lives, you need to disappear," Randy continued but Tyrone laughed sinisterly.

"Let me get this straight. You want me to disappear? I don't see how that's possible. I can't just disappear from my child's life like that."

"Maybe you're not understanding me. I told you we are going to work on our relationship and raise our daughter together. There's no you in this equation."

"Oh, I see. You want me to disappear and act like I didn't exist. That's not gonna happen."

"It's not up for negotiation at all. We want you to leave us alone and disappear. I put together a little something to sweeten the deal so to speak," Randy mentioned before sliding Tyrone a check and a briefcase. And, once he saw the amount on the piece of paper, his eyes almost popped out of his head.

"Twenty-five thousand dollars. Are you serious?"

"There's another twenty-five in the case. So, yes. I'm serious."

Denise looked at her husband in disbelief. She couldn't believe Randy offered Tyrone that much to leave them alone. If she knew Tyrone like she thought she did, he wouldn't be able to resist.

"And, this means what?"

"That you resign from all the positions held at Oakdale then leave the church and my family alone forever."

"I see," Tyrone said as he held the check in his hand.

"Oh. And, we don't plan on telling anyone at the church about this. So, if you even think about it, you'll be sorry you were born." Randy's face became emotionless.

"Is that a threat, PASTOR?" Tyrone chuckled.

"Remember, I haven't been a Christian all my life. Either agree or it's time to move on to my alternative."

Denise sat there for a couple of minutes not saying a word, just taking in everything. She couldn't believe what she heard, never thought Randy was capable of devising something so crooked. It taught her that you can't put anything past anyone.

"Randy, this is a whole lot of money. But, I just don't know if I can do that." Tyrone took the check and slid it across the table back to Randy.

"What's there to think about? I just gave you fifty-thousand, tax-free. With that, you can buy a new family. Just leave us alone. So, here." Randy slid the check back across the table.

Denise smiled as Tyrone folded and stuffed it into his wallet, knowing her husband made Tyrone an offer he couldn't refuse. She knew people were sometimes hesitant to cooperate but the whole game changed once money was added. She watched Tyrone picked up his briefcase and walked out of their house.

"Babe, I didn't expect you to do that." Denise peeked through the curtain and watched as he sped off.

"You didn't expect me to do what? Handle my business?"

"I have to admit, you did. Paying him off was clever," Denise said as she recalled the similarity to her situation with the doctor.

"Well, I learn from the best," Randy said as she turned around from the window with her mouth wide open.

"What do you mean?" she asked, trying to play dumb.

"I know about the money you gave your doctor. So, cut it out."

"How did you find out?" Denise raised her eyebrows.

"After the scene at the hospital, I ran into her. She told me she had something to give me, which was the envelope you gave her. She explained how she couldn't accept it." Randy pulled out the envelope.

"I'm sorry about that too."

"That's the past, Denise. All we can do is move on and work through everything."

"Randy, you have been nothing but wonderful to me. And, this is how I repay you. I am so sorry. I want you to know, I love you." Denise walked toward Randy and put her arms around him. He gave Denise a quick hug and then pulled away.

"I did what I had to do because I love you and Kaylah." Randy forced a half smile and walked up the steps in the direction of the bedroom. Denise was happy to know that even though things weren't completely back to normal, they were at least going in the right direction and could see Randy was glad to have his family back together again.

Chapter Twenty-Two

"Can you believe she's one month already?" Denise asked Randy as she gave Kaylah a bath.

"I know, seems like time's flying."

"Before we know it, she'll be in kindergarten."

"Look at my beautiful baby." Randy kissed Kaylah on her forehead.

Denise stood back as he took over, lifting her out of the tub and drying her off. Seeing him fuss over her made Denise so grateful things were working out between them. Yes, life changed, but looking on the bright side, it was improving day by day. She admitted, for a while, that she didn't know if they would work it out. Even though they did agree to stay together, it was still different. Randy had indeed forgiven Denise but wasn't so quick to be affectionate and wasn't trying to have sex with her even after she had received the okay from the doctor.

Just to get Randy in the mood, Denise went to Victoria Secret and purchased several teddies she hoped he'd enjoy. She even strutted around the house for no reason trying to turn him on, still nothing. It was almost six weeks to the day of Kaylah's birth and she was tired of going to sleep not getting any. Although Denise was frustrated, she figured she could hold out to make sure things were alright between them. She felt keeping her husband was worth her situational celibacy.

"Denise, where's the powder at?" he asked.

"Look over to your right, on the dresser." Denise pointed across the room to the cherry wood dresser that was custom made just for Kaylah.

"Since she's going to be christened today, are we going to put on her outfit now?" Randy lifted up her garment bag securing Kaylah's white lace dress.

"No, I figured I would when we got to the church. Just in case she spits up."

"Good thinking," Randy hung the bag back on the door.

"Baby, if you don't mind finishing up with her, I'm going to get dressed before everyone arrives for breakfast."

"Go ahead. I'll be alright." Denise turned around to walk out the room and Randy grabbed her hand and stopped her.

"Wait a minute! Come back here for a second."

"Yes Randy."

"Before you go, I just want you to know how much I love you. I know you've been trying hard to make us work and I want you to know it doesn't go unnoticed."

"Thank you baby." Denise leaned in and kissed Randy. It felt good so she closed her eyes and absorbed the moment as he planted soft smooches on her lips.

"And, to show my appreciation for how hard you've been working, I have a surprise for you this evening."

"Randy, you know I love surprises. What is it?"

"I'm not telling you. But, I will say this. After we christen the baby today, Michelle and Jimmy are going to keep her for three days." Randy smiled and Denise didn't care where they went as long as it had the word "resort" or "spa" included in it.

She walked down the hall to the master bedroom humming and trying to figure out what she was going to wear to church. She opened up the closet door and decided to put on a new outfit she purchased from Saks Fifth Avenue. She held up the lime green and teal jacket with the matching knee length skirt and figured it would be perfect with her teal Christian Loubotin's.

Thank God I decided to buy this when I did because I have to make sure I'm looking fresh for Kaylah's christening. It's been a little while since I've been at the church and I know some of the lonely, single women have been hanging onto my husband a little too tight since I've been gone, but this outfit alone is going to definitely make a statement that I'm back!

By the time she finished putting on her clothes, Randy held Kaylah while admiring her as she stood in the mirror adjusting her skirt.

"Denise, that looks great on you."

"I'm glad you like it." Denise spun around so he could catch a glimpse of it all.

"Like it, I love it, baby. Let me go put on my lime green so we're matching." He handed Kaylah to Denise then slid his gray and black tie off to put the other one on.

"That looks good, Randy."

"Baby, today as we christen Kaylah, I want this to be a new beginning for us. I want us to really start fresh and put the past behind us."

"I feel the same way you do," said Denise as she finished dressing.

As usual, the deacon and his wife were the first ones to arrive. Shortly after, Michelle and Jimmy as well as Terri showed up. They were just waiting for Randy's parents. Denise made up in her mind that she was not going to let anything, or better yet anyone, get the best of her that day. She didn't know if it would be possible once Mama Tate was added to the equation. But, she planned to give it a try. Once Denise heard knocking at the front door, she knew it was Alice - the only one who preferred to knock rather than use the doorbell. Denise said a silent prayer as she went to answer it.

Lord. Please help me not to disrespect this woman as she comes into my house. Help me not to act like a fool on this beautiful Sunday morning, in Jesus name. Amen. When she opened up the door, Mama Tate stood there looking her up and down as if she was an alien from another planet.

"Oh. It's you," she said.

"Hello Mama Tate." Denise moved to the side. Instead of greeting her, she really wanted to cuss and kick her out but was determined to put her best foot forward.

"You look very nice, Denise. That new outfit looks very nice," Alice continued, leaving Denise surprised to hear a positive comment.

"Thanks."

"Too bad it's not nice enough to clean up all the dirt you've done."

Denise smacked her lips, rolled her eyes, and closed the front door. Oh, no she didn't. *Does she even know how close I am to putting my hands on her? Let her keep playing games, I'll send her to Jesus early. Lord, please.* "Mama Tate, I'm not even going to start with you," Denise responded. "Everyone's in the dining room."

"How nice of you."

Denise walked into the bathroom before joining the group. She was glad about keeping her cool as Mama Tate insisted on insulting her. She picked up her MAC foundation and applied some to her face then put on her favorite Ooh Baby lipglass. Denise was getting ready to apply eye shadow when someone knocked on the door.

"Girl, you ready in there?"

"Almost. What's up? Come in," Denise replied before Terri opened up the door, walked over to the toilet, put the seat down, and sat on it.

"I saw Mama Tate walk in and you wasn't behind her. So, I came to see where you were. Making sure she didn't shoot you and stuff your body in one of the closets." Terri laughed.

"I'm not about to let her bother me."

"You should see her in the dining room, going crazy over Kaylah. Kissing her and hugging her all tight. It's ridiculous."

"I know. She's got to be one of the fakest people I know. That's one of the reasons I can't stand her. If that wasn't Randy's mother, I would've jumped her a long time ago."

"She is fake. She's only doing that to please her son. If he wasn't involved, she wouldn't even be bothered with you."

"You're right, how do I look?" Denise turned around from the mirror.

"Good. Don't even look like you had a baby." Terri smacked her lips and acted like she rolled her eyes.

"I know. God is good." Denise finished and they joined the family in the dining room where the deacon had everyone circled getting ready to pray.

"Lord, we come to you asking a special blessing over the food we're about to receive. Let it be strength to our bones and nourishment to our bodies. And, let me receive my plate first. In Jesus name. Amen," he prayed and his wife hit him in the arm with her red clutch purse.

"What on earth possessed you to say that?" she responded.

"I've been working on that line to put in my prayer for weeks. You didn't like it?" He laughed.

"I don't know why you prayed to be the first. You're always first. Matter of fact, everyone automatically lets you go first because we know how you can get when you're hungry." Randy handed him a plate so he could start the line.

"How do I get when I'm hungry?"

"You're the meanest thing on earth. I've seen you come to blows at several church functions over some food."

"If she had just given me the last chicken wing instead of trying to take it for her greedy self, then it wouldn't have been any problems. I had to do what I had to do." He popped his collar like the young guys did it on T.V. and the videos.

"This is Pastor Tate's house, not B.E.T." His wife took her plate and sat down at the end of the table.

"Holla," the deacon added.

"I'm glad everybody could make it," Randy said when he sat down with a full plate of eggs, bacon, grits, and two pieces of wheat toast.

"We wouldn't miss this for the world," Michelle commented.

"I hope everyone enjoys the food. It took me a long time to cook for ya'll greedy people." Denise made everyone laugh.

"Auntie Denise, do you have some apple juice?" her nephew asked.

"Sure, baby. Let me get you some." Denise got up from the table and went into the kitchen. Her sister followed behind her.

"You didn't have to get up. I would've did it," Michelle said.

"It's okay. This apple juice is for him anyway. Randy and I don't drink it all."

"Always spoiling my kids."

"Those are my babies."

"No. Those are my monsters. Kaylah is my baby. She's the cutest little girl I've ever seen." Michelle smiled.

"She looks just like her mama." Denise pretended to pat herself on the back.

"Denise, I'm so happy for you. Even with everything happening the way it did, God still had a way of working it out. Randy is to be commended for how he's handled the whole situation."

"I know, God is definitely good," Denise said. *If my sister only knew how expensive it was to work it out. She wouldn't even be able to believe it if I told her...*

Everyone left the house and drove toward the church. When Denise saw how many cars were in the parking lot for morning service, she was so glad they had a reserved space. There were definitely more cars than usual so Denise smiled because she knew they were all there to witness Kaylah's christening. Most of the members hadn't gotten the chance to see the baby because Denise didn't bring her out much. She didn't want everybody and their mommas trying to hug, kiss, and hold her. That would've completely pissed her off. She definitely didn't want to cuss out any of the church members. Besides, she knew too many people didn't wash their hands after they use the bathroom and didn't want those types of germs spreading to her child.

Randy took the key out of the ignition and walked around to Denise's side of the car. As she got out, she noticed someone sitting in a black automobile across the street. She felt as though this person watched her but figured she was just being paranoid. All of the drama surrounding Tyrone had Denise somewhat on the edge. But, as each day came and went, she felt more at ease.

She hadn't seen or spoken to him. There was no phone calls, no showing up unannounced, no coming to the church, nothing. Denise was amazed by him taking the money and disappearing. If she knew money would've made him leave her alone, she would've wrote him a check a long time ago.

It just felt good for Denise to go to church and not have to worry about running into him. She finally felt like she had her life back, some freedom. The freedom to be her own woman and live her life the way she wanted to without worrying about him.

"Good morning, pastor and first lady," an usher said as she opened up the door.

"Good morning, sister." Randy shook her hand.

"Oh, she is so gorgeous. I think she looks just like you, Denise," she said as she lifted the blanket covering the baby's face.

"See. I told you, honey," Denise said to Randy as he shook his head in disagreement.

"You're in denial. Kaylah looks like me." He laughed then walked down the hallway to his office.

"Hello Denise," the security guard said as he stood there looking her up and down.

"Good morning," she replied, doing the same thing to him. Ever since Tyrone resigned from all of his positions at the church, Randy thought it would be a good idea to hire security. Denise opened the one arm not supporting Kaylah and gave him a hug.

"I like the way that outfit is fitting you," he whispered in her ear. Instead of responding to the comment, she just smiled and looked directly in his eyes. She knew if she wasn't careful she could get herself in trouble so she took a quick second, closed her eyes, and said a prayer as she slowly moved toward the sanctuary.

The announcement of Kaylah's christening must've spread like wildfire because the whole city of Youngstown seemed to be in attendance. The usher escorted Denise down the aisle and everyone kept peaking to see what the baby had on and praising her beauty. *Like mother, like daughter. I know my baby is gorgeous because she looks like me. It's not like I don't see some of the women rolling their eyes because I'm back in church, and even after having a baby, I still look good. Half of the women wished they looked like me. But it's okay. No matter how hard they try, they can never be me so I'm not even worried.*

As she took to her seat in the second row, her eyes scanned the crowd to see if Tyrone was present. He wasn't.

"Praise the Lord, everybody," Randy said as the congregation rose to their feet and clapped their hands and sang "Praise the Lord" in unison.

"God is good. Isn't he?" he continued. "I'm not going to be before you long. But, I just want to share with you some of the things God has been dealing with me about. It always seems like the minute I think I've dealt with something, God will bring it back around and use it to test me. I thought that when it came to forgiveness, I had it all together. I used to see other people being so unforgiving. Couldn't understand why it was so hard for them to absolve and move on, until God allowed some things to happen in my life that made me realize I was no different than them. He took me through some things I thought I would never go through. And through it all, God has shown me the power of forgiveness. To forgive someone who has done you wrong is comparable to how Christ has forgiven us. He didn't have to he die on the cross for our sins. So, my question to you is this. If Christ can forgive us, then why can't we forgive each other? Just take a minute and think about that. The Bible says, if we forgive others then God is to forgive our sins. Therefore, I challenge you to give someone else a second chance."

The organist played *God of a Second Chance,* which let the congregation know Randy's message was over. There were people crying and hugging each other.

"Now, it's time to do something that I've waited to do for a couple of weeks and that's the christening our baby daughter, Kaylah. Family, can you please join me up here." Randy motioned for them to join him the pulpit. As Denise lifted Kaylah up onto her chest to carry her, all you could hear was "ahh" from the church members who were seeing her for the first time.

"We're so excited for you to witness this special event. It's very important to christen the newborn. We believe that since God has given us this child as a gift, it's important to offer her back up to God and pray for special blessings of protection," Randy continued and Denise handed him the baby.

He began to rock her in his arms then kissed her.

"She is our new beginning, a brand new life. As we christen her today, our prayer for you is... If you're in need of a brand new start, let it begin today."

When Randy said that, several people responded with, "Thank you Jesus!" One woman shouted next to her pew while another praised God so much the ushers went over to fan her. And, just as Randy asked everyone to bow their heads and close their eyes, the back double doors of the church burst open. The sound startled everyone and caused them to turn around to see what was going on.

Denise lifted up her head and opened her eyes to see Tyrone. She looked over at Terri who peered back at her with a shocked face while he started clapping his hands as he walked slowly down the center aisle. It was unclear if he was armed.

"It's so funny how ya'll sit here and hang onto this man's every word like he's God or something. But, it was your beloved pastor who bribed me with fifty-thousand dollars to keep a secret that I can hold no longer. Truth is. I used to be a member of this church as many of you already know but that was only because I tried to get back at Denise for not leaving Randy. See, we had been having an affair for a year and a half and that beautiful baby you see up there in Pastor Tate's arms is a direct result of it."

"Tyrone please," Denise pleaded with tear filled eyes. "Please, don't do this."

"Shut up, Denise. You did this to yourself. You knew from the beginning I wanted to be with you. You went along, saying we were gone be together. But, you had no intentions on leaving him. You played me." Tyrone moved closer to the front. "I even took you back when I caught you messing around with my cousin.

The entire congregation, who was completely silent gasped at once but kept listening as if Randy preached the word of God.

"Come on, Tyrone. This is not the place," Terri said.

"Look, if you leave now. We can discuss this all later," Denise cried out.

"No! Remember when I wanted to talk and discuss it, I was told to disappear. Do you remember?" Tyrone looked directly at Denise then Randy, who appeared frozen, as she shook her head yes.

"All I did was love you! Look what you did to me? You never loved me. All you cared about was the sex since your loving husband wasn't giving it up. Or so you said."

Denise stood there, couldn't say anything, and just cried. Randy remained silent.

Tyrone continued, "All you ever cared about was yourself. You didn't care about me. You sure didn't care for your husband, who you claim to love so much. It's people like ya'll that turn folk away from the church. All ya'll care about is taking the member's money so you're wife could shop all day and keep up appearances. I'm surprised you have nothing to say, Pastor Randy. Had a mouthful when you basically bought my child from me. Your daughter's worth fifty grand, Pastor Tate? Uh, is she?" Tyrone moved in a little closer.

"You really need to take this elsewhere before I call the police." Randy straightened his suit jacket.

"I'm not going anywhere until I say what I have to say." Tyrone lifted up his dress shirt and pulled out a gun.

"Lord! Jesus! Please help us," Michelle screamed.

"I feel like this. If I can't have you, then no one will. The game is over, Denise." Tyrone aimed the gun at her. She closed her eyes and prayed, hoping it was all a dream that would disappear when she reopened them. It wasn't.

"It's all over!" Tyrone cocked the gun and pulled the trigger. The sound echoed throughout the entire sanctuary and caused the congregation to scatter in panic toward the various exits, trying to escape danger.

Denise opened her eyes and saw Tyrone lying on the floor in a pool of blood, struggling to hold on to his life. She wondered who shot him and thought about the security guard. Then, when she looked up and over, she saw the deacon holding a pistol.

With the baby still in her arms, she staggered to the first row of pews slumped down and became overwhelmed with emotion. Her eyes flooded with tears as Randy slowly walked over toward her. Once directly in her face, he stopped and stared with absolute disgust. So confused, Denise didn't know how to interpret his appearance, so she extended her arm thinking he would embrace her. However, he didn't.

"I guess God continues to test me on forgiveness and I can not fail. But, at the same time, it's even more difficult to forget. Come on, let me get you two home," he said as he reached for the baby before she stood and they all walked out of the sanctuary.

JESSICA A. ROBINSON is a fresh, new author from Ohio. She's also one-fourth of a national Hip-Hop group named Carnival who's slated to release their sophomore CD in 2009. She has always been an avid reader but came into the wonderful world of writing by accident. Upon losing her father when she was ten to pancreatic cancer, she began journaling as a form of therapy. The emotions and thoughts expressed on paper turned into short stories and continued to evolve from there.

Coming from such a rich background in the church of having twelve ministers in her family, she writes about the things she's went through and the things people have gone through around her. Her spiritual heritage was the breeding ground for her very own genre, "Church Dramedy."

LaVergne, TN USA
29 November 2010
206736LV00002B/15/P